THE SEAL'S SURPRISE TWIN

SPECIAL FORCES: OPERATION ALPHA

RACHEL MCNEELY

Dear Readers,

Welcome to the Special Forces: Operation Alpha Fan-Fiction world!

If you are new to this amazing world, in a nutshell the author wrote a story using one or more of my characters in it. Sometimes that character has a major role in the story, and other times they are only mentioned briefly. This is perfectly legal and allowable because they are going through Aces Press to publish the story.

This book is entirely the work of the author who wrote it. While I might have assisted with brainstorming and other ideas about which of my characters to use, I didn't have any part in the process or writing or editing the story.

I'm proud and excited that so many authors loved my characters enough that they wanted to write them into their own story. Thank you for supporting them, and me!

READ ON!
    Xoxo
    Susan Stoker

To my dear friend, Kay. I have been blessed to have your friendship for thirty-seven years. I always remember how we met through a mutual friend, and we hit it off from the start. You have been such a support to me through good times and bad. I will never forget the fun and the laughter.

Thanks to:
My editor: Raina Toomey, for showing me how to how to make my story better.

Cover Artist: Pat Dengate, for all your patience with me until we find just the right cover.

To Susan Stoker, who made it possible to get this book and my others published. Thank you so much.

Thanks to Amy Hrutkay for all your assistance in

helping me get all the pieces together for my books. Your smile and kindness come through your emails.

PROLOGUE

"ANAIS, SIT DOWN," ANYA SAID TO HER TWIN. "DO YOU remember the man who came for a session and I had worried about what he said?"

Anais nodded. "Did you go to the police?"

"Yes. But the police detective said I didn't have enough evidence to prove my patient was a dangerous man. I told him that as a psychologist, I thought what my patient told me made him a danger to others.

"He said he'd look into it and get back with me. After three days, I called him back. Apparently, my patient happens to be a friend of this detective and he'd assured the police detective that I was over-reacting."

"Did you show the detective the bullet hole in your car window?"

"Yes, but he said they'd never find the person since the car went by so fast, and I didn't get the license number."

"I can't believe he didn't think it might be your patient who shot at you in the car."

"Too many people get mad and shoot at each other nowadays. There must be some evidence, but it wasn't Steen's car anyway. I've watched out my window after a session, and I saw the car he drove several times."

"What are we going to do?" Anais asked.

"I hate that I've put you in danger, too. If my patient picked a spot to attack from a distance, I don't think he could tell us apart.

"We have to talk to Mom, and then we'll move somewhere far off until the police or someone takes care of this guy."

"That seems rather drastic," Anais said.

"Do you have a better idea?"

"No."

"Then let's talk with Mom. She won't be happy and will want to hire bodyguards for us."

"Why not try that first?"

"Because I reported him, and he'll want to see

THE SEAL'S SURPRISE TWIN

me pay. He's a scary man and will stop at nothing to get rid of me. I know his secret."

"You must tell me what he said that frightened you. I need to know why we're making this drastic move."

Anya paced their living room. She stopped and turned to her twin sister. "You can't tell anyone."

"I understand it's hard to break a patient's privacy. But he's made it necessary."

"In his last session, he said he dreamed of choking women while having sex, only he added at the end, that it wouldn't happen again. He quickly corrected himself and said he'd never actually do it.

"But I don't doubt from his expression that he enjoys the dreams, and if he hasn't already, he'll soon do the act."

Anais shivered. "I don't understand why you like your work. It sounds scary and dangerous."

"This patient is the exception from my usual ones. I'll call a friend who's agreed to take over my other patients to let him know I've decided to leave right away. Go pack, and we'll visit Mom before we hit the road."

"Will you tell her where we're going?"

"No, it's too dangerous. After we're settled, we'll go across into Mexico and send her a letter.

We will use our real last name only when necessary like applying for a job or getting our permits to carry a gun, but to regular people we'll make up a different last name to use. Then if my patient does search for us it'll make it more difficult for him to find us."

"I hate this," Anais said.

"I do, too. But I want us both to live."

CHAPTER 1

Chief Petty Officer Kijika "Shadow" Gibson slipped through the jungle ignoring the bugs buzzing around him. He used all the tactics his Cheyenne grandfather taught him when they hunted, so as not to alert the prey. Remembering his grandfather made him smile. The hunt was a bit more difficult with all the extra supplies he carried, but he'd learned how to compensate.

As he moved closer to the gang's hideout, he stopped and looked through his binoculars. Men roamed around the tents. Some sat by the fire swatting bugs and smoking. None looked like the man they'd come to take back home to face charges. Their reports said he'd left the States to meet with the local leader.

The authorities hadn't known who led the cartel until they'd captured several of his men. They identified him to receive shorter sentences. The team's mission was to bring in the man who headed the drug cartel locally and his American boss.

The American made a big mistake when he had two SEALs captured and executed. Every SEAL wanted this man brought back to America. Shadow and his team were determined to be successful.

I'd like to shoot him, but in many ways, he'll suffer more by facing a trial and going to jail. Killing him would be too easy.

"See him yet?" Jackson, known as Bear to his men, asked Shadow through his earpiece.

"Nope. I have a good view. I'll let you know if he's here."

"We're going to start moving closer."

"Right."

SEVERAL HOURS WENT BY BEFORE SHADOW HEARD AN engine. He moved his feet just a bit to be ready to bounce up when needed. The driver got out of the enclosed jeep and walked to the other side. A tall man stepped out, stretched and glanced around.

Shadow crawled on his stomach closer to hear their conversation. Thankfully, they'd moved back around the jeep and opened the door for another occupant to get out.

"You're hidden well in this jungle. I doubt anyone will find you here," the tall man commented to the driver. He turned to the attractive woman who'd joined them. "What do you think, darling? I doubt anyone will find our operation. See, we have nothing to fear." He rubbed his fingers down her thin neck and across the diamond necklace. "You can still enjoy the little trinkets you get from me."

She moved against his side and kissed his cheek. "You are such a darling."

A local woman came out of a tent on the left side. The tall man told his pampered woman, "Go with her, dear. I have business to attend to, and then we'll return to civilization."

His wife or paramour, Shadow wasn't sure which, cheerfully followed the other woman.

Still smiling pleasantly, he said to the driver, "She has a busy mouth. After I leave, dispose of her."

The man grinned. "Our boss may want to toy with her first."

"Whatever. I need that woman to disappear off the face of the Earth."

7

"Won't anyone miss her?"

"No. I only play with women with no strings, so when I'm tired of them I can see they're gone. This trip gave me the opportunity to take care of two problems at once."

"Come this way. The boss is anxious to see you."

Shadow spoke very softly into his mic. "We have more trouble. Move up."

"We're a short distance behind you. Be there in a few minutes."

HIS MEN HELD BACK AS BEAR MOVED UP BESIDE Shadow. "What's up?"

"He brought a woman with him. He wants her disposed of, as he told the other man."

"Damn. It's going to be difficult to get all three out alive."

"I have an idea she knows too much about his business. She'll be a valuable witness in court."

"Where is she?"

"In the hut right in front of the jeep. He just went into the second hut on the right side."

"Stay here. I'll move back and explain to the rest

of the team. We'll split up and half go left and the other right."

Shadow nodded. "I'll start moving toward the back of the tent on the right. When you or whoever enters from the front, I'll cut the back and come in. It'll help confuse them, and we'll have a better chance at getting them out alive."

Bear nodded and said, "Heath will be coming in from the front."

"Good." Shadow bellied forward into position. He noted several of the men had dozed off in the humid, hot air with their guns cradled in their arms. *Dumb asses think they've got it made.*

The rest of the team moved slowly into place. Shadow knew what to look for and still barely saw the movement of the bushes. Once they were in the clearing, they quickly shot the sleeping men. Before the others got over the surprise, the SEALs charged into the tents.

Ripping the back of his assigned tent open with his knife, Shadow jumped in and grabbed the American as Heath did the same to the local man. Each threw a black headpiece over the prisoner's heads and backed out with them into the brush as the gang ran in the front.

Shadow quickly tied the men's hands and directed them to run with him and Heath.

"Take off this mask," the American demanded. "You don't understand. This gang was holding me as a prisoner."

"That's hard to believe. You greeted your jailers in a very friendly manner. I saw it all. Shut up and run for your life," Shadow said.

He tried to resist. Shadow knocked him out. "Damn it. I ought to leave you behind to rot in this jungle." He threw the man's limp body over his shoulder and headed for the boats the SEALs had hidden upriver. Heath followed behind with his prisoner.

Shadow knew the others would destroy the camp and march to the river to rendezvous with them.

Darkness was falling when they reached their destination. Shadow threw his prisoner down beside the rubber Zodiac and Heath told his to sit. Gordy, who stayed behind to protect the boats, jumped out to help load the prisoners.

"The others won't be far behind. They had to rescue a paramour of his." Shadow nodded toward the man he'd carried through the jungle. "He'd tired of her. She didn't suspect he planned to leave her there. I'm certain she'll sing like a bird when she gets stateside."

"Good work. I hope the others aren't far behind. We need to join the motorboats before daybreak."

The man awoke and started demanding to be released. "Shut up," Gordy said. When the prisoner started to speak again, Shadow bound his mouth to quiet him. "Don't give me any more trouble. Our government wants you back in one piece, but I'd just as soon kill you if I have to."

The local was stoic except for a frown of warning for his boss.

The American struggled with his ropes for a while, but finally gave up. There's was no moon. Good in some ways, but it made it harder to see where to walk. Still, Shadow knew his team would use their GPS and arrive shortly.

When they came through the trees with several other prisoners, Shadow smiled. "It took you long enough," he teased.

The men's painted faces appeared weird in the silvery moonlight. "It's good there aren't any other natives around. They'd swear you were bad ghosts come to get them," Gordy said.

"Let's get these guys and the woman on board

and get out of here before the rest of the group comes after us," Bear said.

When the rubber boats landed on the back of the motorboats, the SEALs took a deep breath and pulled the boat and their prisoners further onto the fast-moving vessel.

"I demand to know why you've treated me this way and where I'm going," the tall American said.

"You'll be handed over to the authorities when we get stateside. It's up to them what happens to you afterwards." Bear turned to the woman who'd been in the jeep with him. Bruises and swelling was clear on her face beneath tear-streaked makeup. "I think she'll be happy to tell the judge and jury about all your crooked deals.

"We also know you ordered two SEALs executed, and your partner here did the dirty work. We're taking you both home to face what you've done."

Bear looked across at the local leader of the gang. "Your government and ours reached an agreement for you to be brought to America to face trial for the killing of our SEALs. I'm sure your American friend here will try to put it all on you. I'd suggest you cooperate. The jury may go easier on you than him."

"I had nothing to do with those Seals' deaths. I'm innocent."

"No, you aren't," the woman spoke up. "I heard you telling someone to execute the prisoners. I didn't know they were Navy SEALs," the woman said. "I wanted out then, but I knew if I didn't pretend I cared for you, you'd kill me."

He gave her a hate-filled stare. "I planned to get some money out of selling you overseas."

Her face went white, and she sat with her head down on her knees. The rest of the trip home went smoothly.

SHADOW SUCKED IN A BREATH OF FRESH AIR WHEN HE arrived back in San Diego and drove to his house and into his garage. He threw his dirty clothes bag in the laundry room. He'd shower, lay on his couch in front of the television and relax with a bourbon and coke.

The cool, clean water cascaded over his body, reviving him somewhat. After dressing in shorts and a t-shirt, he ambled into his living room and flipped on the television. The six o'clock news was on. Too tired to cook, he reached for the phone and ordered a large pizza with everything. Then he went to his bar and fixed a drink.

His attention was drawn to the television when a male reporter said excitedly, "The police negotiated the release of the hostages about two hours ago. After they were safe, the SWAT team rushed in the bank and arrested the men who'd been holding them. They took the would-be-robbers to the police station where the people who'd been held captive are giving their statements."

The reporter moved to block the way of a woman as she walked by him with another woman. "Wait, weren't you two hostages?" he asked and tried to step in front of them.

Shadow leaned forward and blinked. *It couldn't be. No one was that unlucky.* But when the camera moved closer, he saw Anais trying to back away from the news reporter's mic.

Shadow sat down and studied her heart-shaped face. Her blue eyes looked both startled and frightened. The man towered over her short frame.

Anya stepped beside her. "Get out of our way," she demanded, looking quite ready to punch the guy in the nose. He stepped back quickly, and the women disappeared into the crowd.

The reporter shrugged. "I guess they didn't want

to be on camera. Maybe someone else will be more eager to talk."

Energy surged back into Shadow's body. He grabbed his cell phone and speed-dialed Dirk, his best friend on their SEAL team and better known as Ranger.

"Hi, Shadow. What's up?"

"How about coming to my house and having a cup of coffee?"

"Sure, I have time. I'm planning to go to Aces Bar and Grill later. I'll dress first and stop and visit before I join the others. Aren't you going?"

"I may, but I'm tired, more than usual. I'll get ready just in case I change my mind."

Shadow poured the bourbon and Coke down the sink. He needed a clear head. He'd barely finished making a pot of coffee when Ranger knocked on the door. The pizza arrived at the same time.

He paid the delivery guy and asked Ranger to take the pizza to the table outside. He'd get their coffee. "I'll join you in a minute. The sun's setting, and it's nice out there."

"Sounds good to me."

Shadow came through the door carrying two cups of coffee. Ranger stood by the small table set to the side of Shadow's swimming pool. He was looking up at the sky and taking deep breaths of fresh air.

He turned to Shadow. "Do you ever swim? I've never seen you in the pool when I'm here."

"I do. Usually late at night. It's quiet and a good time to relax and think."

"I'm glad you got this house when it went up for sale a couple of months ago. How do you like living here instead of that small condo you rented?"

"I haven't been in the house very long, what with the undercover work and then this last long assignment, but so far it's much better.

"I was waiting for something to become available in this neighborhood, but people around here don't often move. It took longer than I'd expected."

"True. Mostly, it's the older folks who don't want to bother with the lawn and upkeep anymore." Ranger grabbed a slice of pizza. "Tell me what you want to discuss."

Shadow sat in the other chair. Outside the walls around the garden, the noise of children's laughter and the sound of lawnmowers soothed him.

His thoughts went back to his attraction to Anais. It had surprised him. Normally, he liked strong women, more athletic—like Anya—and not the type who'd go around with a gun she couldn't shoot. And yet there was no denying the strong pull between him and Anais.

He had to admire her willingness to brave the unknown, to face any danger to save her sister, her twin. He liked the subdued fire of the woman he'd met the day he'd done what he could to extricate the sisters from a very nasty situation involving a cartel and a shipping container full of frightened young women destined for the sex trade. It was too bad he was undercover at the time and there was little to differentiate him from the bad guys, at least in Anais's eyes.

He'd observed the twins' closely that day and wanted to learn more about them. But then he got a call for a new mission and all his focus was on completing his assignment successfully.

He must have been quiet too long, because Ranger asked, "Are you all right?"

"Yes, I'm just trying to think about how to explain what I want to tell you."

"Just say it."

"I told you briefly about the twins, and how in the normal course of events I'd be attracted to Anya. She appeared tough and smart, and I admired her. But when I met Anais ... she's not at all like the women I usually ask out.

"She didn't know how to shoot a gun, but brought it with her anyway. She seems soft, and kind, and different. I'm puzzled about my reactions to her, but despite that, there's something about the twins' I can't quite trust. And yet I want to."

Shadow had to smile when Ranger stood and started walking around the yard. Ranger got his nickname because he liked to walk around when thinking.

RANGER TURNED AND STUDIED SHADOW. "YOU WERE in a tight spot for many days while being inside that gang. When you see her again, you may not feel the same. People, even guys like us who are used to it, react in strange ways while under pressure. Becoming attracted to a total stranger is not like you."

"I know."

"Uh-huh. So why do I have a feeling you plan to contact them?" Ranger stared at Shadow.

"You know me well. The twins' puzzle me, and I love solving mysteries."

"It might not lead where you want to go."

"True. I have a feeling Anais and Anya are not who they told me, and I want to know why."

"You can walk away and not get involved."

Shadow shook his head. "I wish, but something keeps telling me to find out whether they are involved in something illegal, or if they're in danger for some reason. I believe they're running from something or someone. Otherwise, why would they be so nervous about being on the news? They were hostages at a bank robbery, and often hostages will speak with reporters"

Ranger shrugged. "Perhaps they like to be more private."

"Like us, or like criminals, but who else might get that upset?"

"What do you plan on doing?"

"I asked for your advice."

Ranger walked to the side of the pool. For a minute, he didn't say anything. Then, he faced Shadow with a very serious expression.

"I'd keep as far away from them as possible. You rescued them once. Don't get involved again. The Navy might dislike the idea of you having contact with people involved in a previous case." Then Ranger smiled. "Of course, you won't take my advice, so why ask for it?"

"No, you're right. I won't contact the twins, but if they call me, I may have to become involved."

"You can tell them to talk with the police. Whatever's going on, it's probably the jurisdiction of local police and nothing to do with us."

"And what might you decide if you had a similar predicament?"

"Hell, I knew you'd ask me that. I won't answer. This isn't my decision to make." Ranger finished his coffee and grabbed one more slice of pizza on his way out. "I have to run. It's almost time to join the team."

Shadow walked him to the front of the house and watched as Ranger crossed the street diagonally to his house. Like so many of his SEAL teammates, he'd bought a home in a neighborhood close to the Navy base. Heath, known as Blaze, and Gordy lived two blocks down.

It would probably be a good idea to join the team at Aces. *Otherwise, I'll be too tempted to contact the twins. Ranger's right, I don't need to get involved.*

And yet as he prepared to go out, he listened for the phone to ring—which didn't make a lick of sense, since he'd never given them his number. *Good. They'll have to work to find out how to contact me.*

CHAPTER 2

THE THROWAWAY PHONE, KEPT ONLY FOR CALLS FROM their Mom, rang as Anais cooked dinner. Anya had left the kitchen to shower. "Hello, Mom. What's up?"

"I had the six-thirty national news on and saw the two of you. That reporter said you'd been hostages in a bank robbery. I had to call and make sure you're all right."

"We were hoping it would only be on the local news."

"One man turned out to be a guy that had been on the FBI's top ten list for years. The FBI believed he was living somewhere in Europe. I guess that's why it made the national headlines."

"Damn. I really wish it hadn't. I don't want to move somewhere else. Did they show us clearly?"

"Yes and being twins will make you more recognizable to the man searching for Anya." Her mother's voice hesitated, then blurted, "Go to the police in San Diego. Tell them your fears. Maybe they'll be more agreeable to having someone look out for you."

"Mom, Anya tried that before. We don't have any more evidence now than Anya had the first time."

"I worry about the two of you, and I miss you."

Anais noticed her sister standing in the kitchen doorway, gently rubbing her damp auburn hair with a towel. Anya raised her eyebrows when she saw Anais on the special phone. Anais whispered, "Mom saw us on television."

Anya took the phone and Anais went back to preparing the meal. "Don't worry, Mom. We have an idea about someone who may be able to help us. We'll move from here if we have no other recourse. My former patient probably doesn't even watch the news." She went silent as their mother said something Anais couldn't make out. "Okay, we'll change phones and call to give you the number. This one is being crushed and thrown out."

At the dinner table, Anais stared at her sister. "What can we do?"

"I'm not sure. We don't know how to get in touch with Shadow. He'd have to call us, and after his silence all this time, I doubt we'll hear from him."

"The Navy will never let him get involved," Anais said. "We'd be taking advantage of him if we asked for more help."

"There's no one else we can talk to about this, and he may have new ideas of how we can stay safe."

"Why don't we wait and see if anything strange happens?"

"And while we wait, my patient may be driving or flying here." Anya paced the floor. "How can we find Shadow?"

"Let's make some calls and see if we can find out where the locally based SEALs go on Friday nights to have fun. They must have a place to let off steam."

A couple of women Anais called were going to the movies and invited her along, but they had no idea of where to go to meet guys and dance. She thanked them and hung up after promising to join them another time.

"Have you had any luck?" Anais called out to her sister in the other room.

"No, and I only have one number left to call."

"This will be my third call. I have another

number after this. Let's hope one will be productive."

Anais dialed the number of a nurse she met at the hospital when she got treated for the flu the year before. They'd hit it off, exchanged numbers and gone out to a few movies.

"Hello, Josie. It's Anais."

"How are you, Anais? I haven't heard from you in weeks."

"My sister and I haven't been getting out much." She gave a little laugh. "We're going a little batty. We wondered if you knew a place to meet nice men and dance."

"I do, actually. I had a maternity patient who is a SEAL's wife. He was so handsome and attentive that I asked where I might find someone like him. She told me to go to Aces Bar and Grill. The SEALs fill the place on Fridays and sometimes on Saturday nights." Josie chuckled. "I'm going to Aces this evening. A guy I dated just got back from a mission. Why don't you and your sister come with me?"

"We'd love to. Are you sure you don't mind?"

"Not at all. But you can follow me. I may not go straight home," Josie said, her tone flirty with meaning.

"No problem. We'll meet you at your house and follow."

"Great. See you here around seven."

Anais looked up at Anya, who had come to stand in front of her, and shut off her cell. "I guess you heard. Josie said Aces Bar and Grill is where a lot of SEALs let off steam. And a group just got back from a mission. Maybe Shadow didn't call because he wasn't here."

Anya nodded decisively. "Let's get ready. What time did Josie say to meet?"

"Her house at seven. We'll dump the dishes in the dishwasher and get dressed."

WHEN SHADOW ARRIVED AT ACES, HE SAW RANGER wave to him. Two tables had been put together for Bear's team and Wolf's, as well as the significant others for those men who had them. Wolf's team had gotten back about a week ago from a mission. The mood was happy and a bit rowdy.

Shadow sat in the chair beside Ranger. "Did you break down and call them?" Ranger asked.

"No. You're right. There are too many questions

surrounding them, and our captain might not like me getting involved."

"No serious talk tonight," Marcel yelled and reached across the table to hand Shadow a beer.

Someone else slapped him on the shoulder. "Have fun."

Shadow grinned and raised his beer, "To us. May we always find our way home."

A wave of cheers went up from the wives and SEALs. Shadow noticed the husbands kissing their wives and the tender touch of their wives' hands against their faces or hugs to their arms.

"I wonder how coming home would feel if you had someone waiting?" Ranger said.

"Are you lonely?" Shadow asked.

"Occasionally. We're seldom in town long enough to seriously date and then want to pop the question."

"I suppose you're not talking about asking them to bed."

"No, and you know what I mean."

"There are advantages to alone time. I like to read and do hobbies. If you have a wife, it's like caring for your favorite pet. You'd be required to fix things for them, take them out, talk to them, go places with them whether you want to or not. You know, all the husband stuff."

Ranger bent over in laughter.

"What's so funny?" Shadow asked.

"Your version of comparing a wife to having a pet for companionship. Don't let any woman you might care about hear you describe her that way. Your relationship will be dead in the water."

"I doubt I'll settle down," Shadow said. "When my Dad died, just before he retired from the SEALs, my Mom was overcome with grief. I wouldn't want to put a wife and kids through such a rough time. Being our wives is not an easy job."

Caroline, Wolf's wife, turned to Shadow. The look in her eye made him think there was more than one reason she'd earned the handle Ice. "I overheard what you said. Please don't think any of us"—she nodded toward the other wives—"regret marrying our SEALs. Yes, it's more difficult because of the time apart, but I'd rather have Matthew than any other man. You take the good with the bad." She grinned at Wolf. "And the good is excellent."

Wolf kissed her.

"She's right." The other husbands and wives nodded in agreement.

"I guess you've been told," Ranger teased. He glanced through the crowd to the front door.

"Who are you looking for?" Shadow asked.

"My lady. We started dating a few weeks before we went on this last mission. I called her after I left your house. She agreed to come and bring friends." He grinned. "There she is, waving from the door with two other women." Ranger took a closer look. "I think they're twins. I'll be right back. Move more chairs around the table."

Josie waved at Ranger. "That's my guy. Follow me. They're way across the room."

Anais nodded. She and Anya followed closely behind Josie. "This place is noisy and crowded," she said to Anya.

"And filled with big, handsome men. Maybe we will find Shadow here," Anya said, raising her voice just enough to be heard over the noise.

Ranger met them halfway there, greeted Josie with a kiss and slung an arm around her shoulder. It wasn't until she looked past Ranger that Anais saw Shadow waiting at the table. He'd stood and smiled, but it was different, more polite, not as friendly as when they'd last seen each other.

"Sit, we've added chairs for you three," Ranger said.

"Ranger, these are my friends, Anya and Anais Piercy."

Ranger studied the twins' and looked at Shadow. "Are these the two you saw on television?"

"Yes." Shadow turned to the group. "I met Anya and her sister, Anais, briefly before our last mission. Then today they were on the news. I believe you were hostages in a bank robbery. Am I correct?"

Anya's face had hardened, but Anais blushed. Anais nodded. "We didn't want to talk with that reporter. Who'd believe we'd be so unlucky twice or at least my sister was unlucky twice."

Wolf leaned forward. "This is strange. Is there some explanation?"

"Yes, but we can't discuss it here," Anais said.

Anya snapped. "We might not discuss it with anyone. We'd have to be certain about trusting them."

"That goes both ways," Shadow said.

Wolf held up a calming hand. "I have an idea. We'll stop the questions for now, but tomorrow you and Anais will meet with me, Bear, and Shadow at my house," Wolf said. "You can trust us. But if you tell us something illegal, we'll report you. My wife is writing down our address. If you're not there by noon tomorrow, we'll understand you can't tell us anything. Now, let's have fun."

The guys gave a cheer and ordered more drinks. Shadow moved down several seats until he had Bear on one side and Anais on the other. Ranger had Josie seated to his right and Anya sat beside her. He raised his eyebrows at Shadow before turning to Josie.

"You're angry with us," Anais said in a low voice.

"I'm not sure how I feel about you two. I think there are secrets not known to me, and until everything comes out in the open, I'll be wary of you and your sister."

"Fair enough. I can't blame you. Would you rather we leave?"

"It doesn't matter," Shadow said, and yet the softer feelings he wanted to deny were in his heart when she looked up at him.

Her bright blue eyes had dimmed when he spoke. He fought the urge to take her slim body into his arms and hold her sweet smelling body close.

Involuntarily his fingers brushed a stray lock of her auburn hair off her forehead, and his eyes centered on her cupid-shaped lips. Startled at his thoughts, he moved further from her.

"We won't stay long. If we leave right now, it would seem strange," Anais said.

"I agree. The band is playing a slow number. Ranger and Josie are starting to dance. Shall we?"

"I'd love to, yes."

Shadow knew he was in trouble when he put his arms around her. Her softness and smile made his body ache. *I have to control these feelings until I know what's going on, but right this moment I'm not doing very good.*

"I'm sorry for making you suspicious of us. At the meeting tomorrow, you'll understand why we weren't able to tell you our secret when we met. Although you seemed trustworthy, we still didn't know you that well. I guess the mistrust was on both sides."

"If you and your sister show up and tell us your secret, I'll trust you."

Anais looked up at his lean face. His high-cheek bones and stern expression made her heart drop. He was ruggedly handsome with firm, but sensual lips and a strong jaw. *I'm attracted to him, but will he ever trust us after this is all over?*

When the music stopped, Shadow guided her back to their seats. The waitress placed a glass of red wine on the table in front of Anais's seat.

"I didn't order wine."

The waitress smiled and nodded to Ranger. "He ordered a glass for you and your sister."

Anais looked down the table at Ranger and thanked him. While sipping her drink, she looked around at the other people.

"Are the men here tonight all SEALs?" Anais asked.

Shadow glanced around. "Most. This place is close to the base. When you get assigned duty in Coronado, it doesn't take long to hear this is the local place to drink and relax."

"I'd never heard of it before I talked to Josie. She invited us to join her. My sister and I had called almost all our friends before we found out she knew where the SEALs congregated. We wanted to talk to you."

"Why?"

"I'll explain tomorrow."

"Then you do plan to show up at Wolf's?"

Anais lowered her head and nodded yes. "I hope

Anya agrees with me. She agreed we needed to talk with you, but I'm not certain she'll want others to know our secret."

"I'd have to discuss your problem with my ranking officer before I'd agree to help, so getting Wolf and my team leader, Bear, involved is a good idea. They can go with me to see Captain Buchanan and support the idea." Shadow frowned. "But if this is not legal, we won't touch it."

"Do you think I'd be doing something illegal?"

"I don't know. SEALs tend to be suspicious until they know the truth."

"Then we have nothing to worry about." Anais stood and motioned to her sister. "We'll see you tomorrow."

Anya joined her. Caroline handed them a slip with the address and phone number on it. "Call if you get lost."

"Will do," Anais said. She turned and walked quickly to the side door with Anya close behind her.

Wolf leaned forward to look around the other guys at Shadow. "Seems you made the lady mad."

"Good. Let's see if the two show tomorrow." Shadow took a swallow of his beer and sat back in his seat. He'd finish his drink and head home. He had a lot of thinking to do before their meeting in the morning.

S<small>HADOW PACED THE FLOOR IN HIS BEDROOM</small>. He hated when his feelings and duty seemed to get mixed up. It seldom, if ever, happened. After a swim, where he tried to tire himself out, he showered and put on his shorts. Then he called his mother. It was a bit late, but he knew she liked to sit up and read into the evening.

"Hello, Kijika." She always called him by his real name. "Why are you up so late? I thought after returning from a long mission you'd be in bed asleep."

"I'm sorry I didn't talk with you longer today. How are things at home?"

"I'm fine. Now that I've retired, I've been working in some of the classrooms at school. I enjoy seeing and helping the children. But you didn't call me this late to ask about my day. What's up?"

"You know me well. I'm not even sure where to start. I wish Grandpa were still alive. I miss him and all his good advice."

"Your uncle wouldn't mind taking over Dad's job

of being your mentor. He'd love to see you. You haven't taken a vacation in a long time."

"I know. Something's come up, and after I settle this problem, I'll visit."

"Promise?"

"Yes."

"Mom, when you met Dad was it an instant attraction for both of you?"

"Ah, you have met a lady." He could hear the satisfaction in her voice. "The answer is yes. I didn't want to be attracted to him. I knew from the friend who introduced us that he was a SEAL, and he warned me upfront about his lifestyle of being away often."

"Didn't what he said make you want to step back?"

"No. Once we looked at each other, there was no turning back. I can't explain. I was one of those people who knew right away when she'd met the only person for her."

"What if he turned out exactly the opposite of what you had thought you wanted for a husband?"

His mother laughed. "Oh, my son, he was very different. He reminded me of sunlight, and energy, and lightning. Your Dad brought all of those qualities into my life."

"Looking back, do you regret your decision to marry him?"

"You know better than to ask such a silly question. Of course not. I'd rather have the time we had together than anyone else for a longer time. This lady must have made quite an impression on you to inspire such questions."

"Yes. I feel silly saying this, but from the first time I looked into her eyes, my heart knew she was different."

"I will look forward to hearing an update frequently. It will be better than any book I'm reading."

"What are you reading now?"

"A love story about a SEAL and his lady."

"Oh, Mom, I have to go." He heard her chuckle as he put down the phone.

I'm lucky Dad found Mom. She's the best, and I am going to visit soon and talk with Uncle Maska. He is more like my grandfather than any of Mom's other brothers.

He lay down thinking he'd toss and turn with his mind too busy with thoughts of tomorrow, but he used the ancient meditation he'd been taught to free the mind and was surprised when his alarm went off. He'd slept well, but did remember seeing just as he drifted into sleep a vision of a woman in the

THE SEAL'S SURPRISE TWIN

distance beckoning to him. Was it Mother or Anais? I don't know.

Shrugging, Shadow stepped into a cold shower. It wouldn't be long before he had some answers regarding the twins.

ANAIS AND ANYA FOUND WOLF AND CAROLINE'S house without any problem. When they got out to walk to the front door, Anya touched her sister's arm.

"Remember, go slowly and see how they react to my story before we give them details such as our real names."

"We have to tell all of the truth, Anya. They are SEALs. We have nothing to hide, and they may be of help to us."

Anya frowned, but reluctantly nodded her head in agreement. "I've grown suspicious of everyone."

"That isn't good." Anais started to ring the bell when the door opened.

"I saw you drive up," Caroline said. "Join us in the kitchen."

Anais liked the atmosphere of the sunny kitchen and the smell of cinnamon buns. Her stomach growled.

"I bet you were too nervous to eat this morning. I'll put out the buns and pour the coffee. Unless you'd rather have tea?"

"My stomach is a little nervous. Do you mind if I have tea instead?"

"Of course not. Come over and show me what kind you like."

Anais walked across to where the coffee and a pot of hot water warmed. She picked out an herbal tea with no caffeine.

"I don't need the caffeine. I'm afraid I'd start climbing the walls."

Caroline hugged her. "Don't be nervous. We're all friends here. Sit, and I'll bring your tea as soon as the water is ready." She handed out the coffee to the others. "You are all to relax and enjoy my cinnabuns and your drinks. We'll talk after we finish eating."

Anais had sat by the empty chair hoping it was for Caroline. Her sister sat to her left and Shadow was right across from her. She glanced his way. For once, she couldn't read his expression.

The room stayed quiet as they ate the buns and drank their coffee and tea. When they'd finished, Caroline quickly cleared the table with Anais's help.

Wolf smiled at the two sisters. "I can feel the tension in the room, but believe me, we want to help.

If we can. Jackson or Bear, as we call him, meant to be here today, but something came up. He's Shadow's team leader."

"We aren't doing anything illegal," Anya snapped.

"Anya, tell them what has happened to us. Start with talking about your patient."

"Are you a doctor?" Shadow asked.

"A psychologist. I had my own office in North Carolina until we had to flee the state." Anya stopped and took a deep breath. "This is difficult for me. Only a few people know where we are and why we left home. I trust you will not tell anyone who might put us in danger."

"We will only explain to Captain Buchanan if it looks like we may be able to help you. If you were frightened enough to flee your home, why didn't you go to the police in North Carolina?" Wolf asked.

"I did. The detective said I didn't have enough information for them to do anything. I think he and my former patient were friends."

Wolf nodded. "I see. Please, continue with your story."

They both talked at different times, explaining what happened, their fears, and the current fear that Anya's patient might have seen them on television.

"Mom called. She said the story of the attempted bank robbery had been on national television, and she saw us," Anais said.

Shadow looked across the table at Anais. "Are you using your real names?"

"Only when necessary. We changed our last name. We wanted to keep our real first names. Our family name is Kenly."

"Did your father and mother agree with this plan?" Caroline asked as she got up to refill their cups.

"Dad died five years, before this all happened." Anya held her head between her hands and looked down.

"Anya and Dad were very close," Anais explained. "I loved Dad, but Mother and I were not as interested in horses as we were of painting."

"You paint?" Caroline looked around at her.

"Yes, some."

"Is your mother Dacey Kenly?" Caroline asked.

Both Anais and Anya smiled.

"We tell Mother that she's known everywhere, but she doesn't believe us. Wait until I tell her she's known in California," Anais said.

"What's she known for?" Shadow asked.

Caroline turned to him. "She paints the most

beautiful pictures of old houses and flowers in the field. Pictures that make you ache for the old times and a place like that to retreat to when needed."

"You paint also? Or you did?" Caroline asked Anais.

"In the past it was mostly a hobby. I have sold some paintings. There's quite a pile of canvases to put up for sale when this is all over.

"My real job is as a physician, an internist. I haven't checked on the rules about applying to work in California as a doctor because we may not stay here. I do volunteer work at the hospital. It keeps me from going crazy."

"Damn, you two are not at all who we thought, and what a surprise." Shadow stared at them.

"What we've told you is the truth. Do you have any ideas to help us become our real selves again?" Anais asked.

"Did you go to the local police here?" Wolf asked

"I did," Anya said. "They were sorry, but couldn't help. I wanted them to know my story in case something happened to one of us. There's always the chance he'll hurt Anais thinking she's me. I hate that I've put her in this position."

"You won't have any peace until this ends," Shadow said. "Wolf, will you and Bear go with me to talk with Captain Buchanan and see if we can help?"

"We will. I'll call and tell him about your situation." Wolf looked at Anais and Anya. "I have a buddy who's a SEAL stationed on the East Coast. He owes me a favor. I'll contact him and see if he can find out whether this guy is still in North Carolina or headed this way. Write down this guy's name and occupation."

"He's well-known in our little town," Anya said. "He's a councilman. I think that's why the police didn't believe me and wouldn't get involved. His family's lived in the area for generations and is well-known." Anya took the paper Caroline handed her and wrote down her former patient's name and address.

"This will give the men a place to start," Caroline said. "But in the meantime, I think you need to live somewhere else. We have an extra room where people have stayed for a short time."

They both shook their heads at the same time. "Thanks," Anya said, "but we feel safe where we are. We have lots of outdoor safety lights and alarms connected to 911. We also have plenty of supplies so we can lie low." She stood and put her chair in place.

"We'll go. Thanks so much for listening to us and believing us. Please let us know what you find out."

Shadow walked around to Anais's side. "You need to learn to use a gun and more about self-defense. I'll pick you up later today after our talk with Captain Buchanan. We'll go to the shooting range, and I'll give you your first lesson on how to handle a gun." He looked over Anais's shoulder at Anya. "I expect you are well-trained."

"Dad wanted to teach us both, but Anais wanted nothing to do with guns. I'm fine."

CHAPTER 3

CAPTAIN BUCHANAN LISTENED AS WOLF DESCRIBED the meeting with the twins.

"And what is it you want to do?" Captain Buchanan asked, looking from Wolf to Bear to Shadow.

Wolf spoke first. "We'd like to find out if this person is still in North Carolina. I have a SEAL friend who can check on the situation for me."

"If this guy isn't there, do you plan on trying to find out his whereabouts?"

"Yes, Sir. If it's all right with you." Shadow leaned forward. "I have mixed emotions regarding Anais and Anya. What they said sounded truthful, and why would they lie about any of this? But I am emotionally attracted to Anais. I want you to know about my personal feelings from the start."

The captain sighed and shot Shadow's team leader a rueful glance. "Bear, all your men seem to become involved with women in trouble."

Bear grinned. "Including me, Captain. See how well my lady and I worked out."

"True. Still, my superior is going to start asking questions one of these days. Such as why you all end up marrying the women you rescue." Buchanan grinned, then sobered. "This is the time for you to rest and relax before another mission."

"If we don't help, we'll worry, and that's worse. We're used to being in the middle of the action," Bear said.

"All right. I agree you can see where the man is at this time. Talk to me before any further involvement."

"Yes, Captain Buchanan." They saluted and hurried out.

"Join me at my house, and we'll discuss our plans," Bear said.

Shadow and Wolf agreed and headed toward their vehicles. Shadow called Anais before starting his engine.

"Hi, I'm going to a meeting. It shouldn't last long.

I'd like to take you to a gun range and start the lessons."

"I'd rather not."

"I'll be with you. You'll be safe." There was silence on the other end. "Anais, are you still there?"

"Yes. Shall I bring my sister's gun?"

"No, I'll stop and buy the gun that's best for you to learn on."

"Why are you insisting on teaching me to shoot?"

"Because this man sounds dangerous. I want you both prepared to protect each other."

"All right."

"I'll call when I'm close to your house."

I suspect there's more to her being afraid of guns then she's telling me. At least she agreed to try and learn to use one. Why am I attracted to a woman afraid to learn how to protect herself?

When Shadow got to Bear's house, Kayla met him at the door. "Bear and Wolf are in his study. Go on in."

He knocked and went inside. "Sorry I'm late. I called Anais about training her to use a gun."

"Good idea," Bear said.

"Not to her."

"I called my buddy in North Carolina," Wolf said. "He'll drive to the twins' hometown and check around. The general public should know if one of their council members is out of town. Gossip flows easily in places where everyone knows each other," Wolf said. "He'll also try and find out if anyone has any idea where the twins' are at this time."

"Probably some of the people besides her mother saw them on the news," Shadow said. "It might help us to know whether what they told us this morning is the whole truth."

"Do you doubt them, Shadow?"

"I'm not sure. Something makes me wary, even if I'm attracted to Anais. Maybe because I am. She's not the type of woman I'd normally pay attention to."

"Wolf, if your friend does find out this guy is headed our way, what do we do if the Captain tells us to mind our own business?" Bear asked.

"What we've done before. We'll find a way around his order only if the twins' are in immediate danger."

"I agree." Bear said.

Shadow nodded. *But I won't stand by and see them harmed. I can't.*

"I'll see you two. I want to buy a gun Anais won't be scared to use. Her sister's gun is threatening. I'll buy her a small pistol and work up to one that will do real harm."

"Sounds like a plan. We'll be in touch if my friend finds out some important news," Wolf said.

WHEN SHADOW LEFT, BEAR GLANCED AT WOLF. "WE both know he's not going to obey the Captain if the order is to stay out of the twins' business. Captain Buchanan will probably tell us to step back and have Anais and Anya go back to the police."

"You're not wrong. Shadow won't obey that order, and our teams will not leave Shadow all on his own."

"Right."

"WHAT AM I GOING TO DO?" ANAIS ASKED HER SISTER. "He can tell us apart, so you can't switch with me. We might be able to fool a lot of people by switching clothes, but not Shadow. He saw the few differences from the start."

"Tell him the truth."

"That I know how to use a gun and ways to protect myself? He already had doubts about us. If he finds out we've lied about something else, he might tell the others, and then they'll refuse to help us."

"It's not exactly a lie. It is true you don't enjoy guns and knives and all that. Dad had trouble getting you to let him teach you the same lessons I loved."

Anais shook her head. "I lied to him when he caught me. That story about being helpless went over well. After all, I had no idea he wasn't one of the gang members who held you."

"You did what you had to do at the time. Shadow can't hold what you said then against you."

"Yes, he can and will. I'll try and pretend I'm a beginner. When all of this is over, I'll tell him the truth. We can't lose his or the SEALs' support now. We need them."

"Anais, he may not forgive you."

"I know, but I have to think of keeping you and me alive." Tears came into her eyes and rolled down her cheeks. "I know it's too soon, but I like him, a lot."

Anya held her sister tight. "If you get out there and change your mind, it's okay."

"I won't. If it were only me, I'd confess, but I will not put your life in danger. We need him and his friends' help. Keeping up this part of the charade is a risk I have to take. I wish we'd told him about me when we had the opportunity at Wolf and Caroline's house."

The ring of their doorbell made them both jump. Anais glanced out the living room window. "He's here." She opened the door and smiled.

Shadow walked in and glanced around. "I see you have a security system to view who's outside, but you didn't speak with me before opening the door."

"I expected you and recognized you. If you were unknown to me, I'd have asked for identification."

"Always do it. Someone might have a gun on me and be hiding in the bushes. If you spoke to me, I'd have had a chance to say something that would make you suspect a problem."

"Smart. I hadn't thought of that," Anya said from where she stood behind Anais. "What's in the box?"

"A gun for your sister. Starting with a small pistol won't be as frightening for her as your large gun."

"Very considerate," Anya said. "The afternoon is moving along, and the gun range where I practice closes at five. You'd better get on your way." She motioned for them to leave.

When Shadow got into his truck after helping

Anais in, he asked, "Why was your sister so anxious to get rid of us?"

"She likes her alone time and hasn't got much of it since her kidnapping. We've both been staying close to home."

"Open the box and take the gun out. Get the feel of holding it. Don't worry. I didn't load it."

Anais almost smiled. It was a small pistol. Trying to act dumb just got more difficult.

At the gun range, Shadow started by showing her how to load the gun. "Now you do it."

Her hands were shaking from nerves as he watched her, and she dropped the bullet. "How stupid of me. I'm sorry."

Shadow bent and retrieved it. "Your hands were shaking. You must be very afraid. Did something happen to put this much fear in you regarding guns?"

"I think it's all the news you hear and sometimes people shoot people they love accidentally."

"When I finish with my lessons you'll be confident that won't happen."

His understanding smile and kindness made her feel more guilty for her deception. "I'm sure you're a good teacher. Let me try again." This time she put all the bullets in the chamber. "There, I did it."

"Good. I'll shoot first."

She watched his stance and admired how his body naturally went into position, and he fired. Then he handed her the gun and stood behind her.

"Put your arms out and let me control your position. Look down the barrel of the gun. See the target?"

"Yes."

"Pull back the trigger and shoot."

At the last minute, after he'd let go of her arms, she let her hand quiver just enough so she didn't hit the bull's eye, but it hit inside the target.

"Great. You're a natural. We'll have you hitting the bull's eye in no time, and then I'll teach you how to use a gun more like your sister's.

"I did it." She handed him the gun and threw her arms around his neck. "Thank you."

"We're not through yet. You have to learn to sight the target without my help."

Having Shadow watching her closely made Anais nervous, and it was easier to pretend to have trouble hitting the target. But by the end of the lesson, she gave up the pretense and hit the bull's eye.

"Wow, you are going to be my best student. I think your eye and hand coordination is much better than some others I've taught. Congratulations. Let's get something to eat. You can call Anya and see if she wants to join us."

"I will." Anais moved a few steps in the other direction to make her call.

Shadow packed the gun safely in the box and checked to see they'd left the range as they had found it. Then he walked over to speak to the man practicing beside them.

"Anya, I did well. He wants to take us out to eat. I'm exhausted from two hours of pretending. Please join us."

"All right, but where are you going?"

Anais waved to get Shadow's attention and asked where Anya could join them.

"There's a small restaurant by the water about halfway between here and your house. Tell her to drive toward the gun range. She'll see a place called Seaside Grill. We'll meet her there."

Anais relayed the message and clicked off her cell.

Shadow took her hand on the walk to the car.

"The Grill has good seafood. They also have dart games we can play with your sister."

"It sounds like a great way for me to relax."

Shadow glanced her way. "You relaxed quicker than I thought you would."

"I know. It surprised me, too. But it's such a little gun. Not as threatening as the guns and rifles my Dad used when he tried to teach me to shoot." Every lie that slipped past her lips made Anais feel worse.

Shadow leaned down and stared into her face as he opened the truck door. "You look upset. What's wrong?"

She forced a smile and told another lie. "I'm fine. I'm just hungry. I didn't eat lunch."

"If you'd told me, I'd have stopped on the way." He lifted her into the truck. "We'll order an appetizer right away when we get to the restaurant, while we decide what we want for our main meal."

"You're too nice to us." Anais turned to the window and looked out as they drove along.

"You are very quiet. Did your first lesson tire you out? I noticed you were nervous."

"Perhaps, a little. I'll feel better after I eat."

"I hope each lesson gets easier for you."

Anais took a deep breath. She was not normally a liar. Ane each one she said to Shadow made her feel like she was sinking deeper and deeper into a hole.

"You didn't go to sleep on me, did you?"

Forcing a smile, she turned to face him. "No, I was admiring the scenery." *Any moment now lightening is going to strike me for telling all these lies to this wonderful man who wants to help us.*

"There's Anya. She must have left the house right after I called." A sense of relief swept over Anais.

Shadow led the two into the restaurant. He asked the waiter for a table in the back. Smiling at Anais, he said, "They have a waterfall and a beautiful garden you'll enjoy."

When they got to their table, Shadow arranged to have them face the garden. It gave him the chair against the wall.

"Don't you want to see the garden?" Anais asked. "We can shift our chairs where you'd have at least some of the view. It is beautiful."

"No, I always sit facing the door. It's a SEAL thing. We like to know what's going on around us."

"Even at home?" Anya asked.

"Most of the time."

"Anya, come with me to the restroom." Anais smiled at Shadow. "We'll be right back."

"Don't rush. I'll order an appetizer for us."

As soon as they walked through the door, Anais checked the stalls to be certain they were alone, and then she turned to her sister. "I'm ready to tell him the truth about my skills. I can't stand lying to him."

"I suggested you tell him. The only problem is he and the others may refuse to help us. But I'm okay with us taking that risk."

"Their Captain may not let them help us anyway."

"You're right. We've already told Shadow and his friends all but that one part."

"I'm going to discuss it before we order our main meal. Shadow may walk out. If he does, I won't feel like eating anyway."

"Okay, sister. Let's go face the dragon." Anya tried to make it a joke, but it fell flat. Anais frowned and left the ladies room walking with a determined stride toward their table.

Shadow stood as they approached. "The appetizer just arrived. I ordered a mixture since I didn't know what you'd prefer."

"It all looks delicious," Anya said, as she sat in her seat. Anais moved her chair so she sat directly in front of Shadow.

He looked puzzled. "I thought you'd sit beside me."

"Normally, I would. But I have something to say,

and I'm not sure how you will handle the information."

Shadow wrinkled his forehead. "Surely you aren't afraid of my reaction. I'd never hit a woman unless she was going to hurt people I love or my country."

"I never feared you'd get physical." She lowered her head.

"I think I know what you're going to say."

Anais looked up and stared at him. "You couldn't."

"You didn't need my lessons today. I suspect you can protect yourself with your sister's gun, too."

Anais felt the air whoosh out of her lungs. "I'm sorry we didn't tell you. There was so much to discuss yesterday." She tried to smile. "We left that part off. When you called, I didn't want to tell you over the phone."

Shadow leaned back in his chair and studied both sisters. "I thought we'd cleared the air, and now I wonder what else you may have conveniently not told us."

"Nothing." Anais's throat tightened to keep back her tears. "When you confronted me the night you all rescued my sister, I didn't know what to say or who you were, so I lied about myself. It was silly. If you'd been one of the bad guys, you'd have taken me to the place where my sister was being held and put me there with her."

"I need to think, and I'll have to report this to my captain. He'll make the final decision about helping you. Not me. Excuse me."

He stood as the server arrived to take their order. "Put their bill on my credit card," he told the woman as he handed her his plastic. "Something's come up. I have to get back to work."

"No, we'll pay," Anais said. "It's the least we can do."

Looking puzzled, the waitress handed his card back to him. "Whatever," he said and quickly exited the restaurant.

Anya took the menus. "We may as well eat."

"I don't think I can."

"Yes, you will eat their delicious food. You're losing too much weight."

"I'll give you some time to decide," their

waitress said. She rushed off toward another table.

"She probably thinks we're all weird," Anais said.

"We are." Anya smiled at her sister.

CHAPTER 4

"Do you think they're hiding anything else?" Captain Buchanan asked Shadow.

"Anais and Anya were nervous yesterday and may have honestly felt better leaving that information off. But why didn't they tell me as soon as I arrived today?"

"Were they surprised when you realized Anais was trying to fool you?"

"Anais came back from the restroom and told me the truth. So I don't think she knew for sure I'd guessed what she was going to say. I expect she took her sister with her to let her know she planned to tell me all of it."

"I think you're right to be wary of them. But we

can't forget what they told you about the one sister's patient. They may be in danger."

"Will the commander stop us from helping?"

"I'm not going to mention it unless things develop where it's necessary. Keep me up-to-date at all times. I've already discussed this with Bear and Wolf."

"Yes, Captain. I will let you know what's happening."

Shadow's cell rang as he walked out the door. "Hi, Wolf. What's up?"

"I heard from my friend. Are you on base?"

"Yes."

"Meet me at the cafeteria. We can talk. I'll ask Bear to join us."

"Sounds good to me. I missed lunch. See you there." Shadow put his cell back in its holder and got in his truck. He hoped whatever Wolf's friend had found out would help clear up some of the questions he had about Anais and her sister.

SHADOW WAS THE FIRST TO ARRIVE, SO HE GRABBED A sandwich, ordered fries, and got his drink. He strode over to a free table in the left back corner and placed his tray on it before going back for the fries and a piece of coconut pie.

He had started to eat when he spotted Wolf and Bear. He lifted a hand to signal them. They nodded and grabbed their own coffee and pie before joining him.

Wolf took his first bite and smiled. "They do have the best pies. I always have trouble deciding between the lemon or the coconut."

"I see we all have one thing in common," Bear said. "We got the coconut."

They talked about their families and Shadow mentioned his mother. "I want to plan a visit with her and my uncles. It's been a while."

"What's happening with the twins?" Wolf asked.

Shadow explained the latest information.

"Anais was the one right beside you at Aces, right?" Wolf asked.

"Yes, why?"

"She did seem more nervous than her sister. So what if she does know how to shoot a gun and other ways to protect herself." He shrugged. "I'd bet she isn't as comfortable with weapons as her twin. Her sister is the harder one in that pair."

"Maybe that's why Anais attracted me rather than Anya. She seemed softer to me, too."

"Still," Bear said. "She's not your usual type."

"We've finished eating," Shadow said to stop further conversation about him and Anais. "Wolf, what did your friend discover?"

"Quite a lot. It's a small town full of gossip. Most of the talk was about the councilman leaving for Florida and not returning. It seems the wife thought he'd gone off on a solo vacation, which puzzled the people who knew him. They said the two had always gone on vacation together.

A few said they wondered if he left to get away from his wife. One man, who identified himself as the councilman's friend, said the councilman planned to ask his wife for a divorce. He was waiting for the right time." Wolf took a gulp of his coffee.

"My friend talked to a police detective. He mentioned the psychologist who reported the councilman and his fantasies. Apparently, the detective laughed and told my friend that he didn't put much stock in therapy. It surprised him that Girard Steen wasn't seeing her. And the detective added that she was good-looking. He said Steen probably was leading up to asking her out, and she got offended."

"Wow. The town sounds backward when it comes to how they think about women," Shadow said.

"I want to send Ranger and Taylor, who was better known to his team as Hawke, to Florida. This councilman's wife told everyone he was going to the panhandle to fish. Let's see if they can find him or anyone who's seen him," Bear said.

Wolf spoke up. "One more thing. Right after the councilman left, the wife's best friend was found dead under mysterious circumstances. The sheriff and his detective are being very quiet about how she died."

"I grew up on a ranch near a small town, but it was nothing like this one," Bear said.

"You're from out West. It's a different region of the country."

"Is that good or bad?"

Wolf grinned at Bear. "Are you going to fight me if I say bad?" he teased. "You know it's good."

"Okay, you're off the hook." He turned to Shadow. "I'll notify and detail the mission to Ranger and Hawke and tell them to fly to Florida. I doubt they'll mind this assignment. Sunny skies, beaches with pretty women in bathing suits, and lots of good drinks."

"We have to get back to work." Wolf picked up his tray. "Shall we meet at my house tonight for a beer and barbecue?"

"Will Caroline mind a sudden influx of guys?" Shadow asked.

"No, she loves having you all over to eat. I'll call her as soon as I get back to the office."

When Shadow got to the beach, Hawke walked over to him with a big grin on his face. "I expect you may have heard about our new assignment. Best mission I've had in two years."

"I can't wait. We're leaving now to get our flight to Pensacola." Ranger said.

Laughing, Ranger and Hawke ran up the beach toward their cars in the parking area. Shadow joined the others. They all had to keep in good shape, so workouts on the beach were typical. Afterward, he told them about the invite to Wolf's house. They separated to get cleaned up for the barbecue.

When Shadow got home, the place seemed quieter than usual. But then, he hadn't spent much time here in months. He'd gone on two missions, one almost right after the other. He showered, put on shorts and paced around his room, stopping by the phone on his dresser several times.

Finally, he opened his cell and dialed Anais's number. She answered immediately.

"Shadow. I hoped you'd call."

"I wanted you to know the man you and your

sister fear has supposedly gone to Florida. Two of the men on my team are flying there. They'll check to see if that's where he went on vacation and if he's still around. Until they report back, you and Anya need to stay home and be alert and careful. I'll ring as soon as I know something certain."

"Thanks, we appreciate the help."

Shadow hung up knowing he'd left a lot unsaid, but he didn't know what he wanted to say. He walked to the mirror in the bathroom.

I want to go to this little town myself and talk to the wife and the police. But I'll have to wait and see what Ranger and Hawke find out.

He shrugged and looked at his watch. *Time to dress and go to Wolf's to talk about how to keep the twins' safe and catch this guy.*

For a second, he thought about Anais, and then he shook his head. *I can't let my feelings get involved until I know for sure they have told us everything.*

Wolf greeted Shadow at the door. "You're early, but so is Bear. I'll grab a beer for you. Bear's in my man cave, as Caroline likes to call it." He grinned and headed toward the kitchen. Shadow joined Bear.

"How are you doing?" Bear asked, his eyes knowing. Though they'd just seen each other a few hours earlier, his next words proved he knew what Shadow had been wrestling with. "I understand how confused you can get when dealing with a safety problem and you have emotions for the lady in danger."

"I'm going to try and cool it until I know they've told us everything. I'm hoping what I discovered today is the last secret." He shrugged. "So Anais can shoot as good as her sister. I also suspect they both know some martial arts."

"Which I doubt will help them if this crazy guy surfaces."

"I'm hoping you'll hear something from Ranger and Hawke by tomorrow or the next day. I've told Anais and her sister to stay safe in their house, but if it takes too long to hear from them the twins will want to go out. They both miss their work."

Wolf walked in with the beer and some snacks. "Caroline fixed some snacks for us. Do we know how to recognize this guy?"

"Thank her for us," Bear said.

"Oh, I will," Wolf grinned.

Bear glanced at his cell. "Ranger messaged that he looked at the Councilman's local town paper online before they left for Florida. There was a picture of Steen, so he copied it."

"Good."

Shadow said, "I was considering going to this guy's town incognito and seeing what I might find out.

"Let's wait until we have more information about this guy's whereabouts," Bear said. "He may be headed this way or already here. You're impatient because your feelings are involved."

"Okay, you're right."

"After this is over, I want you to go home and visit family," Bear said. "I can tell when you need that grounding."

"Really?"

"Yes."

"You're a smart team leader. By the way, the others will be here shortly."

"The grill's hot and ready."

RANGER AND HAWKE CHECKED INTO A MOTEL IN Pensacola. They unloaded the rental car and Hawke sprawled across the nearest bed.

"This is pretty comfortable. I hope our theory is right and this guy came to the big city first. We can ask about where the good fishing takes place," Hawke said.

"They have one of those books for tourists on the dresser. I'm going to thumb through it and see where the popular watering holes are around here. Maybe our guy is a talker when he's had a few drinks."

"Did you bring your bathing suit?" Hawke asked.

"I thought we'd buy something more Florida style in one of the stores. We can always ask if anyone has seen our buddy. We were supposed to meet him at the local motel, but he checked out a few days ago. How's that sound?"

"Good to me, but I'm not wearing a suit with decorations on it or bright colors."

Ranger laughed. "I imagine they save those for kids and young girls."

"I hope so."

He paused in his page flipping to say, "There's a restaurant listed here that's located by the beach. It sounds like a good place to eat and ask about our friend."

"Fine with me. I'm hungry, since we didn't get much food on the plane, and then it took more time getting the rental car."

"Remember, we're SEALs. We can do without food for long periods," Ranger teased.

"Yes, but this isn't a trip in the jungle or up mountains."

"I never pictured you for a whiner."

Hawke shoved him. "Fuck you. Let's go eat."

Ranger chuckled on the way to the car. It wasn't far from the restaurant, and they were early enough to get a good seat by the water. A pretty young waitress came to take their order.

"We'll have the shrimp appetizer and the chips with melted cheese. My friend is starved. "We'll look over the regular menu while you get those and two beers."

She started to walk off when Hawke said, "Wait." He pulled out the picture of the councilman. "We were to meet another friend at the motel where he told us to check in, but he wasn't there and hasn't been.

"We're wondering if he got a room somewhere else nearby. Do you recognize the man in this picture?"

The waitress looked closely at the newspaper clipping. "I don't, but I'll ask some of the other servers. I'll bring the picture right back."

"Thanks, we appreciate it. We're getting worried about him," Ranger said. When she walked off, he turned to Hawke. "Good idea and story. It'd be nice if we got some info on him right away, but I doubt it'll be that easy."

When the waitress returned with their appetizers, she brought the picture back. "I'm sorry, no one recognized him. I showed it to the bartenders, too. The police station is down a few blocks if you're really worried that something might have happened to him."

"We'll look around first and check some other motels and hotels before we involve the police. Thanks for your help."

Once she left them, Ranger said, "After we eat, we'll call Bear and let him know what we've done so far." He grinned when he saw Hawke had already eaten three shrimp. "Leave me some."

ANAIS FINISHED IN THE KITCHEN AND WENT INTO THE family room to talk to Anya. "It's been four days since Shadow called and said his team members arrived in Florida and were looking for your crazy guy. I don't know about you, but I'm going stir crazy staying inside this house."

"If we go out, we may get killed. We have to wait until Shadow says it's safe."

Anais walked around the room. "I miss the hospital and my volunteer work. Hell, I miss being a doctor. Why don't we go out and see if anyone strange comes around us?"

Anya stood and stared at her twin. "I think you're losing your mind."

"Maybe. I'd call Shadow, but we don't have his phone number."

"We have Wolf and Caroline's number. Call them and ask for Shadow's number."

"Good idea, I will. From my bedroom."

Anais glanced at her bedside clock. It was nine o'clock. *Maybe I'll wait until morning. First thing in the morning, I'll call and talk with them. I guess Shadow is putting distance between us.*

She walked to the window and looked out at the wall that surrounded most of the house. She'd liked it there when they were able to go out during the day, but tonight it was another reminder of how her world had changed and not to the good.

Anais forced herself to shower and dress for bed.

"Tomorrow, I'll start another painting. Before this is over I'll hate painting," Anais whispered to herself.

Anya peeped in her sister's room and saw she'd dressed for bed and was sketching on a pad, which she always did before starting a new painting. "Do you feel better?"

"Not much. I didn't make the call. It was too late. Tomorrow morning, bright and early, I intend to talk with Wolf."

"Good, that's better." Anya sat on the end of Anais's bed. "I'm sorry my problems upset your life. I know you miss seeing patients and all that involves. I saw you taking some courses online the other day to keep your license current."

"It's one thing I can do. I don't want to take the boards again."

"You did well."

"Yeah, but it's been a while, and they aren't fun. Don't feel bad about all of this. You didn't cause it. Your crazy patient did."

"I don't like the word crazy; people are mentally ill."

"Do you think he is?"

"I think he's a scary man who has awful urges. I doubt mental health services will change his obsessions. My meetings with him didn't make a difference. Eventually, he'll be caught and put in jail. After this experience, I promise I'm going to do something different. Being twins, my life affects you negatively and that's not fair."

"You love your job."

"I have some ideas for another career. After I mull it over, I'll tell you."

Anais walked across the room and hugged Anya. "I'll love you no matter what happens or what you do."

CHAPTER 5

Shadow's first phone call that morning had been from Anais. As he expected they already wanted to get outside and go to work. He'd told them to be patient. He had to talk with his captain.

He'd only had time to drink half of his first cup of coffee when he got the second call. When he saw it was Ranger, he quickly answered.

"Hi. Any new information?"

"We just talked to Bear. He said to call you. We've combed the town and driven to several smaller places, and to places where people rent boats and get bait. No one has seen this guy. I think you'd better consider he may be headed to San Diego or is probably already there."

"All right. I expect Bear is setting up flights for you."

"Yes. He wants us in Coronado as soon as possible."

I'll talk with Bear and see if he has a new idea."

"See you soon." Ranger clicked off.

He didn't have a chance to call Bear before his cell rang again. "I hate these types of mornings," he grumbled.

"Hello, Wolf. What's up?"

"Your lady called me. She said she and her sister are going back to work. Well, she doesn't exactly work, but volunteers at the hospital, and her sister works at a home for battered women. Apparently you told them to be patient and that didn't work, so they called me. There was no talking them out of it. They said they'd have their guns with them. I gathered both have licenses to carry a concealed weapon."

"Yes, and they both know how to shoot."

"I'm sure you heard that Ranger and Hawke will be back soon.

"Yes. Ranger called me after speaking with Bear."

"Good. Perhaps this guy has decided not to bother the twins. It's been quite a while since they left their hometown."

"I hope you're right."

"I'll see you soon. Captain Buchanan wants everyone here for the morning meeting, and if you don't hurry, you'll be late."

"I'm leaving now."

Wolf cautioned. "See you do. The captain has his eyes on the clock."

Shadow called Anais on his drive to the base. "Hi. I understand you talked with Wolf," he said when Anais answered.

"I knew you'd call, but we won't change our minds. We or me, at least, are going stir crazy. You caught us just before we left. I have to do some productive work. Painting isn't enough."

"I can see there's no changing your mind. Be careful. My men didn't meet anyone in the panhandle area that recognizes your guy. He may be here in San Diego."

"It's a big place. Hopefully, this man who wants to get my sister will never find us."

"'Hopefully' being the important word. I'm off to work. Have a good day."

Shadow put his shoulders back and moved his head around to loosen the tension. He held up his ID as he went through the gates. A busy day at work was just what he needed. He'd be too busy to worry about women who didn't take their safety seriously. *I'll ask the captain to let me off in time to meet them at their workplaces.*

Anais enjoyed her day at the hospital. She ate lunch with Josie.

"I didn't realize you and your sister already knew some SEALs," Josie said. She stared at Anais before taking a drink of her tea.

"Sorry, I ought to have told you the truth. We were trying to get in contact with Shadow about something. We'd met, and I'd given him our number, but we didn't have his. When he didn't call, I thought he'd changed his mind about being interested. But then my sister and I realized he might have been away on a mission."

"Yes, he's on the same team as Ranger."

"Are you interested in him?"

"I might be, but I'm trying not to lose my heart. It's difficult to know if Ranger likes me a lot, or if I'm just a woman to enjoy when he's in port. I didn't go to his place the other night. I told him I didn't want to be a hanger-on."

"What did he say? If you don't mind me asking."

"He said maybe we ought to cool it. He wasn't ready to get serious."

"I'm sorry it didn't work out for you two."

"Don't be. I want someone to look at me and love me like Kayla's husband looks at her and loves her. How are you and Shadow doing?"

"Not so good. We'll see how the future goes."

"Don't give up yet." Josie smiled and glanced at her watch. "Back to work for me."

"And me, too. I'm helping in the nursery today. I love it."

"You ought to study nursing. You'd be good."

"Maybe." Anais wondered how her friend would react when she found out Anais was an internist. The day went by quickly. She checked out of the volunteer office and walked outside. She hoped Anya was already waiting for her in the parking lot.

She saw their car and hurried toward it. Suddenly, a large sedan swung into the parking area, driving fast. Anais moved closer to the parked cars to let the car go by, but it swung directly at her.

Suddenly, Shadow was there, gun in hand. "Anais, get between the cars!" He shot at the oncoming car, but it didn't deter the driver. The car swerved toward Shadow. He shot again before rolling across a parked car's trunk to avoid being hit.

He jumped down, but the sedan had already gone over a curb to get around the pay barrier at the exit and raced away to the west, tires squealing. Luckily it wasn't visiting hours and only a few people were in the parking lot. They'd ran into the hospital screaming.

Shadow ran to Anais. "Are you all right?"

It took her a moment to answer. Her hands felt cold and her voice trembled as she said, "Thanks to you, yes. But the car almost took you out."

"I knew what to do when the person aimed the car in my direction."

Before Anais could respond, Anya was there, jerking her into a tight embrace. Her face was white but her voice steady as she reported, "The driver wore some type of hood over his head and had pulled it forward to keep his face covered. Could you tell if it was our man?" Anya asked.

Shadow muttered a curse. "No. It wasn't even clear whether the driver was a man or woman."

"It must have been Girard Steen. Whoever else would want to hurt us?" Anais glanced toward the road where the car had disappeared.

"Yeah, it must be. I see the security guards running toward us. Tell them what happened. I'm going to search the area."

Shadow frowned when he walked around the other vehicles. *Not a damn piece of evidence on the ground or under the closest cars, and yet my neck is tingling like it does when something isn't right. My grandpa would say to watch for such warnings. They're trying to tell me something.*

One of the guards walked over to him. Shadow introduced himself and explained as little as he could to satisfy him.

"It's good you were here. We need to write this up. Will you all come with me to my office and complete the paperwork?"

"Yes." Inwardly Shadow groaned. He knew they'd report it to the police and there would be more questions.

"Why are you frowning?" Anais asked.

"I hope this proves you need to stay at home. We have to go inside to make out reports and talk with the police."

"Maybe some good will come of this," Anya said. "It brought the person out. We know he's in San Diego."

"And we know he wants to kill the two of you," Shadow said dryly.

"Maybe not. My patient didn't attack me as I waited for Anais. He'd know it was Anais leaving the hospital in a volunteer outfit. People in town thought it was funny that my twin became a doctor, and I can't stand the sight of blood."

"Perhaps he thought you'd suffer more if he killed Anais and you had to live with the thought that it was your fault. You said this guy has a twisted mind."

Anya looked ill. "I never thought of that, Shadow."

"We still need to protect you both. Your angry patient may want to kill both of you. Would he expect you to be carrying guns?"

"No. Anais always leaves hers at home, but I kept mine with me, but hidden. And," she frowned at Anais. "I'd have remembered my gun and shot at him."

"The car came around the corner fast. It happened so suddenly. My mind went blank, so even if I'd had my gun on me I wouldn't have reacted quickly enough," Anais protested.

"Your sister's right. We need to work on the reaction skills of both of you. It doesn't matter how good you are using a gun. In dangerous situations, the person who reacts faster wins."

Anya grinned at him. "I'm so glad we met you."

"I'm not sure how I feel about it. You are two

hard-headed women. There was no reason to put yourself in danger today. Let's get this paperwork done, and then, I'll follow you home, see you're locked in, and I want a promise you'll stay there until we say it's safe to go out."

"Oh, all right, but I did enjoy today," Anais said.

"Me, too. The staff and women were glad to see me at the women's shelter."

"I'm sure they were, but not tomorrow."

Later, when they got to the twins' house, Shadow checked it thoroughly and the locks as he left.

Anya turned to her sister. "I'm glad he's here in San Diego. The SEALs will find my ex-patient, and we will get our lives back."

"I hope we're still alive to get back to a normal life." Anais turned and walked down the hall to her bedroom.

"DAMN, IF YOU HADN'T BEEN THERE, THIS CRAZY GUY would have gotten them both," Bear said. He and Wolf and Shadow were sitting in Bear's home office. Shadow had called Bear as soon as he left Anais and Anya.

"Something is troubling you," Wolf said.

"Just a thought."

"Share it with us." Bear leaned forward in his chair.

"Why did he have that crazy hood over his head? No one knows him here."

"He's smart. You'd have seen him if he hadn't disguised himself."

"True."

"But you don't think that's the answer," Wolf added.

"No. I know it's crazy, but I got that feeling I get when something's not right."

"I've always believed in your feelings regarding danger and such. Did your neck tingle?" Bear asked.

"Yes. I called Captain Buchanan on the way here. He's going call the police and let them know what happened and why I had to shoot at the car. Maybe they'll take him seriously."

"I hope so. He doesn't want us to keep getting involved in local problems when we're at home. Still, I can't stand by and not be involved. I think I may have found the woman for me."

Bear sat back in his chair and whistled. "Wow, I never thought I'd hear you say those words. You've always said you'd never marry and put a wife through what your mother had to deal with when your father died."

"I know. It was especially hard because Dad was retiring in forty days. She'd finally relaxed, and then the worst happened."

Wolf shook his head. "It's all happening too fast to know your true feelings. We'll take care of this guy who wants to kill the twins. Then you'll have time to get to know her and see how it goes."

"I know you're right. But let's make plans to get this guy and keep them safe until we do."

Damn, I thought I had them. I'd kill Anais when she walked out of the hospital, and then get Anya with my gun. But this miss won't get me down. I have everything I need to wait them out. They'll stay at home again for a while. No need to hurry. I have all the time in the world.

I want them both, but if I have to choose, I'll kill Anais. Anya will grieve herself into her grave. Tomorrow, I'll drive out of town to get my arm looked at. Who was that guy? They were lucky a visitor happened to be there and knew how to shoot.

The memory of the gunman calling Anais by name brought a frown. *I have to find out who he is.*

RANGER AND HAWKE KNOCKED ON SHADOW'S DOOR shortly after he left Bear's. "Come in. I'm glad to see you two. You made good time back."

He led them into the living room, where they all grabbed seats.

"Hawke wanted to get home. He's not a good travel companion," Ranger said with a grin.

"I'd be fine, but,"— he nodded his head toward Ranger- he never wants to stop and eat."

"I know a better nickname than Hawke for him. I thought of it on our way back and looked it up in the dictionary. It'll be perfect for him. 'Raven, a bird that prowls for food and eats greedily.' The first night in Pensacola we ordered an appetizer of shrimp. He ate three while I talked to the waitress."

Shadow had to laugh. Hawke looked ready to punch Ranger, but then he started laughing, too.

"I like it. But I already have a name I like better. So cool it."

"I gather Bear can't send you two out together again. At least not here at home. You behave better

85

when you're both hungry, and there's nothing much to eat."

"How do you stay in shape and not gain weight when we're at home?" Ranger asked Hawke.

"I have a good metabolism. I sometimes lose weight when we're home. We do hard exercises every day. I may have to worry about my weight if I ever retire to an easy chair."

"All right, you two. Tell me everything you found out in Florida. Don't leave out anything, no matter how trivial. Well, you can skip telling me about how you two didn't get along."

Shadow sat back and concentrated on what they said about the search. "How much area around the Panhandle did you cover?"

"Most of it. After we checked out Pensacola, we drove around several days and made quick stops at fishing areas and camps." Ranger looked away and then back at Shadow. "We both had the feeling we were on a wild goose chase. We don't believe he was ever there."

"You may be right." Shadow told them about that morning's incident in the hospital parking lot. "They want to go out during the day. I'm going to request one of us accompany them whenever they insist on an outing or going to work."

"Will Captain Buchanan agree? He mentioned when we first got back to rest up because we might get another mission soon. I have a lady I want to see. Although she may not agree to see me anymore." Ranger got up and paced the room. "I think she wants a commitment. I'm not ready."

"Then forget her for now." Shadow got up from his chair. "Bear wants me to go with him to see Captain Buchanan. Do you two want to ride with me?"

"No, you always stay longer. I'll ride with Hawke."

"Raven was a good name," Hawke said. "Maybe it'll fit someone else."

WHEN THEY GOT TO THE BASE, BEAR AND SHADOW told Captain Buchanan about the conversations they'd had with Ranger and Hawke.

"I like that the guys are beginning to think more about nicknames, Captain Buchanan said. "It's time all of you had one. It helps cement the closeness of the team." He cocked his head toward the other side of the door. "I hear laughter. Ranger must have told the team about trying to name Hawke, Raven."

"Can we have enough SEALs to keep the twins' safe? Bear asked. "Since this guy is here, we can find him and end this quickly, I hope."

"You'll have to. The higher-ups are in the process of deciding whether we'll send a team to the Middle East. Bear, I know you just got back, but your team has been chosen to go. The commanders are trying diplomacy first, and you all know how that usually ends. Be ready. Make a plan to keep the sisters safe when your team's gone on their mission."

The captain motioned for them to leave. "Bear, you and Shadow set up a plan for the rest of the time we're here, and let me see it. With any luck, you'll get this man quickly. He can't be smarter than my SEALs."

WHEN THE DOORBELL RANG, ANAIS JUMPED. SHE slowly walked to the door. "Who is it?"

"Shadow."

"How do I know if you're alone?"

"Go to your window and look out."

Anais pulled the curtain to the side. She looked all around Shadow and didn't see anyone. At the door, she opened it but kept the chain fastened.

"If I wanted to get in, that chain wouldn't stop me," Shadow said. "I'm going shopping today for one of the new types of locks where you can see who's at the door before letting them inside."

She released the chain. "I think it's a good idea. Perhaps we need spotlights that come on and show if someone's outside."

"That's the type I planned to buy." When he got inside, Anais threw herself against his body and wrapped her arms around his waist.

"I hate being scared. If only I were like Anya. She gets angry instead of frightened."

"I'll teach you some protective moves to help you feel safer and more confident. Both of you are coming with me to the gym."

Anya had clearly heard his last statement as she joined them from the kitchen. "Take Anais. I know how to protect myself much better than her."

"We'll see. You go with us today. If what you say is right, I'll leave you home after this first visit."

"All right, but you're wasting time on me. I'm a tough chick."

"And yet you got captured by a gang that planned to sell you overseas," Shadow reminded her.

Anya blushed. "It won't happen again, but I guess you're right."

"I've often wondered how they captured you."

"When I leave work, I have my keys in my hand and keep myself alert to others around me. That day, one of the women I'd become close to handed me a card as I left the office. Instead of waiting until I was in my car, I opened it. Someone hit me, and I stumbled. Then another man got on the other side and hustled me into a van. I tried to fight, but they quickly tied me up and gagged me."

"See? No matter how ready you believe you are, someone will find a way if they want you."

"Then why bother with these lessons?" Anais asked.

"Because I'm also going to teach you about being aware always when out in public. It's a mindset you can learn."

"We'll change into our exercise clothes and be ready in a few minutes." Anya urged Anais down the hall.

Shadow moved through the house assessing any vulnerable spots. They'd done well on the inside. They had extra good locks on the windows, but the doors all needed the better locks and the garage was vulnerable. He had his garage made safer. He checked the number in his cell and called to have the work done soon on the twins' garage.

When they returned, Shadow had to smile. Anya looked eager to start, but Anais frowned.

"I'm trying to protect you," he said and put his arm around her shoulder. She turned into his body and hugged him.

"I know. I want to live somewhere safer and more peaceful. I hate all this crime and violence. Before this happened to Anya, I didn't realize how your feeling of safety can get turned upside down.

"No wonder Dad insisted I learn to use a gun and some of the defensive moves he taught Anya. He didn't have any sons, but he said girls needed to have the ability to fight off attackers, the same as boys."

She tipped her heart-shaped face up at Shadow, and her sky-blue eyes stared at him. He knew he'd find it difficult to forget her after this was all over. Without thinking, he lowered his head and kissed her. She put her arms around his neck, and her slim, sweet body moved against his. For a second, he forgot where he was and deepened the kiss.

The sound of Anya clearing her throat brought him to an abrupt awareness. He moved Anais's arms from around his neck. "We need to get started on your lessons." He heard the huskiness in his voice, and his heart pounded in his chest.

Winking at him, Anya headed out the door. "Wait," Shadow yelled.

Anya dropped to the ground just as he heard the bullet. Shadow ran out and to the curve. He aimed at the same car that had tried to run Anais and him down. It was flying down the street. His bullet shattered the back window as the car turned out of sight.

He ran back to check on Anya. She held her hand against the side of her head. Anais was already on the phone and had grabbed a first aid kit from somewhere.

She turned to Shadow. "It may be a more serious injury than it looks. Anya needs the bullet wound area checked in the emergency room to be certain it didn't cause bleeding inside or other serious problems. I put a temporary bandage on and called 911."

Shadow took out his cell and called Captain Buchanan.

"What's up?"

"Anya got shot in the head by a driveby on her way out the door. I yelled at her, but she'd already stepped outside. It appears to be a superficial injury, but she'll be checked at the hospital. The ambulance is on the way."

"Did you get a shot off?"

"Yeah, I busted the back window, but whoever it was kept driving. I had to go back and check on Anya."

"I'm coming to the hospital to join you. I want to go with the sister to the local police."

"Right, see you there."

SHADOW DROVE ANAIS TO THE HOSPITAL AND SAT with her while they checked out Anya. He held her hand and silently cursed himself for giving into his emotions and consequently not realizing Anya's intention to head out the door first. *For someone who says she knows how to protect herself that was an unwise move, but still ... I wasn't as observant as required with these two.*

"You're frowning," Anais said.

"Kicking myself for not taking better care of you and Anya." He was glad to see Captain Buchanan entering the waiting room, effectively putting a stop the conversation.

"Anais Kenly, I'd like you to meet Captain Buchanan."

"I'm very sorry to hear about your sister," Captain Buchanan said and took her hand.

"Thank you. I wish the doctor or a nurse would hurry up and tell me something. I know it didn't look too bad to me. Still, I'd like to have another doctor's opinion. I'm sure Shadow has told you about my sister and me."

"Yes, he has. I'd like you to go with me to the police. I think they will believe your lives are in danger after this episode. The Police Chief returned yesterday from vacation. I'd planned to call him. We're fairly good acquaintances. With you and I both there to talk with him, he'll move your case to a top priority."

"Oh, wonderful. Thank you very much."

A man in scrubs and a white coat appeared in the doorway. Eyes landing on Anais, he asked, though it must be obvious, "Are you Ms. Kenly's sister?"

"Yes. How is Anya?"

"I'm Dr. Andrews. We've done several tests. The bullet didn't enter the skull at all. She's fine. Hurting a bit and I prefer to keep her overnight, just in case something we don't expect happens. I doubt it will, but we like to be extra careful. The bullet that hit her was from a high-powered gun. Not a regular rifle or small pistol. Do you know who shot her?"

"No," Shadow said. "But we plan to find out. I'll stay here with her while these two go to the police."

"We have to report gunshot wounds. The police are waiting by the nurse's desk to talk with you after I leave. Maybe they'll put a twenty-four hour guard on your sister's room," Dr. Andrews said.

"I'll insist when I talk with the Police Chief. I'll explain to the police here that we're headed to the police station. Miss Kenly, are you ready to leave?"

"Can I see my sister first?"

"Sure," the doctor motioned for her to come with him.

"I'll go with them and stay with Anya until other protection can be set up," Shadow said. His captain nodded, sat down, and took out his cell.

Dr. Andrews pulled back a curtain in the treatment area. "They'll have a room for her very soon. I've suggested we get her out of ER just in case. We don't want her attacker to come in here."

"Hopefully whoever it is won't be that crazy."

"You never know these days," Dr. Andrews said and walked off down the hall.

"Anya, I'm so glad you're going to be all right."

"Speak softer, Anais. I have the worst headache.

"But no serious injuries inside your head," Anais said and smiled. "I always said you were more hard-headed than me."

"I'm sorry Anya." Shadow moved closer to her bedside. "I wasn't paying attention."

"You'd turned around before I charged out the door. It's all on me. And I'm glad my sister has found someone who likes her."

"I do, but I'm a person who travels very much in his job, not the guy to be around all the time when needed."

"We'll see. I think you may be perfect for each other."

Shadow shook his head. "I can't make promises."

He didn't look at Anais to see how she responded to what he'd said.

"I have to go, Anya. Shadow's Captain knows the police chief. We're going to talk with him." She didn't look at Shadow or say goodbye as she walked around the curtained cubicle.

Anya frowned at him. "You hurt her."

"Better now than later. I'm going to stay with you. The doctor's afraid your shooter may come in here."

"He'd have to be an idiot, and my patient may have powerful obsessions, but he's also very clever.

Shooting me at my front door seems out of character, but perhaps he's getting impatient."

"Maybe." Shadow sat in a chair close to her bed.

The police officers came to her room and asked questions. When they left, Anya went to sleep.

Shadow's senses had always been keener than most people's, and his instincts had him on high alert. Something wasn't right. Surely, the twins' weren't hiding more secrets.

CHAPTER 6

W HEN THE POLICE OFFICER CAME TO RELIEVE Shadow, he called Captain Buchanan to confirm. "Did you get protection for Anya and Anais?"

"Yes, the evening shift officer for Anais is driving her to the hospital and will take her home after her visit with her sister."

"I'll stay here and see her. I'm going to sneak into the house by the back driveway. I'll check it out. If it's like I think, no one will know I'm there. I suspect this person might try and trick the police guard. If so, I'll be inside to get him."

"Do you think that's necessary or is this a case of your protective instincts for the woman you care more about than you'd like to admit."

"If I didn't have my instincts warning me of danger, I'd agree with you."

"You're seldom wrong when you feel danger."

"I'm going downstairs to meet Anais and her guard."

"I'm having a meeting at eight tomorrow morning with Bear. We want you there, too."

"I will be." Shadow clicked off his cell and headed for the elevator. He'd wait for Anais and her police protector and tell them about his plan.

They were coming in the door as Shadow came out of the elevator. Shadow walked over to meet them. He explained his idea. The police officer frowned.

"It's not necessary. Are you insinuating I'm not responsible enough in my job, and you have to help me out?"

"I meant no offense."

"Well, I'm offended."

Anais put her hand on the officer's arm. "He's overprotective about me."

"Well, I heard he was with you and your sister when she got shot. He didn't stop that person."

"It's a man who has a grudge against my sister," Anais stated firmly.

"Well, who's it to be, him or me?" the officer

asked. "If you don't need me, I can be of more value out patrolling the streets."

"No, I want to have police protection." She nodded toward Shadow, "He's not able to be there all the time."

"You heard the lady," the officer told Shadow, then said to Anais, "Let's go see your sister and then get you safely to your house."

"I'll see you tomorrow," Shadow said and walked out the front door.

Shadow walked quickly to his car. *I have no intention of leaving Anais safety to the police officer. I can sense something is not right. I'm going to her house and try to get in unseen.*

Shadow parked his car at a large shopping center three miles from Anais's home. He wanted to run, but walked briskly to keep from drawing attention to himself. When he got to the street where the twins' lived, he strolled further to get a look at the back of the houses. There was a narrow drive behind them and high walls on both sides. Most walls had a doorway, probably for deliveries. He checked both ways and walked quickly down until he was almost certain this door was behind the twins' house.

The texture of the wall was rough. It was easy for Shadow to peek over. He climbed up the

100

middle section of the wall so the neighbors wouldn't see him. Then he jumped down and moved along the side of the house checking for an unlocked window. He found a small one in the family room. Once open, he barely slipped sideways through it.

I'll look for the opening to the attic. No telling when Anais and the police officer will walk in. I'd have trouble explaining why I was here.

Shadow checked the garage first, and the opening was in the ceiling. He'd just settled in the attic when he heard voices.

"Do you have stairs to your attic?" the officer asked.

"No. We were going to have some put in, but haven't yet. There's nothing up there but an old dresser and bed springs."

"Still, I need to check it. Your boyfriend accused me of not being capable of keeping you safe. I plan to prove him wrong."

"He's a friend, nothing else."

"Hah. He has that look. I can't blame him. I'd feel the same way about my woman."

"I am not his woman."

"Let's see if I can get up there by using the hood of your car." He climbed onto her car and managed to move the lid off the opening. Then the officer pulled himself up and looked inside.

"It's dark in here. Oh, here's the string for the light." He pulled it.

"What do you see?"

"Nothing, your light is burned out." He closed the opening and climbed down. "I doubt anyone would try to hide in there. If they did, they'd have a good chance of falling through the roof, and we'd have them for sure. Let's check the rest of the house."

Shadow took a deep breath. He'd hoped the officer wouldn't notice the light bulb was twisted back just enough not to work. He waited until he heard the front door open and the officer tell Anais he'd be right outside if needed.

"Relax, no one's in the house."

"I'm going to eat and go to bed early."

"Good idea."

Shadow slipped down quietly and waited in a dark corner until he heard Anais leave the kitchen. He'd give her time to get in bed before using his kit to open the locked kitchen door.

I must be insane, but my body is tingling with warnings of danger.

ANAIS SHOWERED AND PUT ON HER NIGHTGOWN. *I'D have liked for Shadow to guard me tonight. Officer Owens seems nice enough, but this patient of Anya's is smart and determined. He's willing to wait until we make a slip like Anya did when she rushed out ahead of Shadow. I'm not a bit sleepy.*

She reached for the radio on her nightstand, flipped it on a tuned it to the station that played easy listening music. Then she switched off the light.

Suddenly, a male figure jumped in her bed and placed his hand over her mouth. He soon had Anais's arms and legs controlled with his body.

The familiar scent of him had her relaxing before he whispered, "Don't scream. It's me, Shadow." Slowly, he moved his hand.

"What the hell are you doing here?"

"I'd hoped for a warmer reception," he said, a twinkle in his eye in the glow of the radio.

"You didn't trust poor Officer Owens."

"No, I don't. Owens was too sure of himself and cocky at the hospital."

She started to move and realized she felt his body heat through her flimsy nightgown. "Get off of me. I'm almost naked."

"Doesn't bother me. Does it you?" His warm hand cupped her chin, and he lowered his head to kiss her. "I want to make love with you, but if you prefer, I'll get back under the bed."

Anais tried not to smile. "Don't be silly. Neither one of us would sleep with you on the floor under me."

"It does seem a waste for me to sleep there."

"I want to make love with you, but I fear the consequences."

"I have condoms."

She chuckled. "Not that repercussion. I'm on birth control."

"Then what?"

"You are a SEAL. I've heard when you leave no one knows the time or where you're going, and no one is certain when you'll return. I imagine their wives and girlfriends have a lot of alone time."

"They do, and I'm not talking marriage, more steady girlfriend."

"Ah, you'll have your fun and sex, too, when you get home."

His expression changed. He looked more serious than Anais had seen him, except when they were in danger.

"It's not fun. We do dangerous work and might

not come home at all on some mission in the future. But we protect our country and our families. It'd be nice to come home to someone special. That's as much as I can promise. If you want me to, I'll go hide in the living room, and you can sleep." He'd moved his body away from her to give her a chance to think more clearly.

Anais reached out and ran her hand up his back. "For some reason, I'm more attracted to you than any other man I've known. If one of them had given me a choice like you just did, I've have shown him the door. For some reason, I can't do that to you."

He'd turned to face her, and she put out her arms. Shadow removed his clothes in a minute and placed a condom on the bedside table. When he climbed back into bed, he pulled her gown over her head and then lay beside her.

"You are beautiful." He nuzzled her neck. "And you smell good, too." His teeth ran across the edge of her earlobe, and then his lips kissed her neck down to where her heart raced.

"You want me. Your pulse is fluttering fast."

"Don't brag. Any red-blooded American woman would want you. But you might be a disappointment. I haven't seen the full action yet," she teased and grinned when he raised up and looked down at her. Her nipples tightened with only a smoldering glance from him.

"Lady, you challenged me. Whatever follows is all your fault."

"Oh, I hope so."

Shadow kissed her neck, the shallow spot above her clavicle, and then blew his hot breath across her nipples. She squirmed under him.

"You like that?"

"Yes," she said breathlessly. "But don't slow down."

"I'm taking my time as I would with a delectable meal, so I can remember each taste and bite." He ran his tongue across her nipples before moving down.

She pulled on him to move back upward. "I want to play some."

Then he heard the noise of the front door opening and stilled. "Shh." In a voice barely louder than a breath, he said, "The front door just opened. You locked it, right?"

Wordlessly, she nodded.

"I'm going under the bed." He moved off the bed and away, silent as his namesake.

Anais quickly found her nightgown in the covers, pulled it on, and waited breathlessly as she heard doors open outside her room. She turned to her side and tried to look asleep. Hopefully, this was the police officer checking everything, though why he'd come in without knocking or how he'd opened the locked front door, she had no idea. Footsteps came closer to the bed. His flashlight shone on her.

"I know you're awake." Officer Owens' voice rumbled in the dark. "I see you breathing hard. Roll over."

"What are you doing in my bedroom? I told you I wanted to sleep. Hearing your footsteps awakened me and scared me."

He sat on the side of the bed. "I got lonely outside and thought we might pass the time more quickly together. You can sleep when I'm through with you."

"Get out of my room." *Where in the hell is Shadow?*

"I will, just before dawn when my relief officer is due to replace me. Move over."

Anais rolled over quickly and reached beside her bed, fumbling for the drawer. Before the officer stopped her, she'd pulled the trigger of her gun, sending a bullet into the ceiling. The shot rang loudly in the room.

"Get out."

He laughed and started to lunge for her hand.

"I'd obey the lady if I was you."

"How the fuck did you get in here?"

"Watch your language around my lady. I let you go longer than I wanted to, but now I have all I need on the little recorder I carry at all times. The Chief isn't going to like what he hears."

The police officer threw himself sideways and then toward Shadow. Another bullet rang out, and the officer fell back, holding his arm.

Shadow held his gun toward the police officer. "Call the police, Anais. Tell them they have a rotten egg in their group, and we have him controlled. But before you call, get me some rope. I saw some in your garage. I'm going to tie him up and then check the locks again."

She rushed down the hallway and through the kitchen. She'd almost thrown out the rope she'd had wrapped around the box when she emptied it a few weeks ago, but now was glad she hadn't. After she gave it to Shadow, she called the police station. They put her through to the officer in charge. Once he heard what had happened, he yelled for two police cars to go to her home.

"I'll contact the Chief. He'll want to know about this."

"Thanks." She turned to see Shadow checking windows and doors. "Where is he?"

"Tied up like a pig going to the slaughterhouse. Owens knows his fellow officers aren't going to go easy on him. He begged me to let him go this time. I laughed and walked out."

It wasn't long before they heard multiple sirens heading in their direction. Shadow had dressed and moved Owens out to the hallway near the living room. "Go get dressed, honey. I'd prefer all those men didn't see you in your nightclothes."

"Thanks for reminding me. I'd prefer it, too." She ran up the hall as the first car stopped in front of the house.

Shadow unlocked the door before they knocked it down.

"Who are you?" the first officer asked. Both of them and the two standing behind had their guns drawn.

"I'm the one who tied up your guy before he hurt Ms. Kenly."

"He's lying!" Owens yelled from the hallway where Shadow had dumped his bound body. "He didn't like me from the start. I don't know how he got in, but he did and was in the bedroom with Ms. Kenly. I thought he had planned to attack her, so I bolted at him."

The police surrounded Shadow and started to release the officer.

Anais appeared in the doorway of her bedroom, tugging a shirt down over the waistband of her jeans. "Don't untie him. Everything he told you was a lie. He came into my room and tried to attack me sexually. I grabbed my gun and shot at him. I missed. Chief Petty Officer Gibson arrived in time to shoot him and get him off of me."

"She's lying."

"My recorder will tell the truth," Shadow said. "I was in her room. I didn't trust Officer Owens, and my suspicions were right."

The sergeant frowned. "You happened to have a recorder on you?"

"It's small. I carry it whenever I consider I might need it for evidence."

"Hmm, this sounds a bit fishy."

"Stand down, Sergeant," the chief said when he walked inside. "Ms.Kenly, I'm sorry, that this officer tried to accost you."

He kicked Owens' foot. "I just heard a rumor yesterday, but the person didn't know which officer was involved. I'd never have thought it was you. You showed such promise." He glanced at an officer standing nearby. "Get him out of here."

The chief turned to Anais. "Will you trust our other officers to protect you and your sister?"

"Yes. I realize this is not a reflection on most police officers. Bad apples can hide almost anywhere," Anais said and smiled.

"Thank you."

Shadow stepped forward. "I'll watch out at night for her and her sister when Anya comes home. At least, I will until I can't be with them because of my job. I appreciate you having them covered during the other time periods."

"I will, and if we haven't solved this problem by the time you have to leave, we'll cover the whole twenty-four hours."

"Good. I have to go now."

"Tell your captain what happened."

Shadow nodded, kissed Anais and hurried out the door.

This time he ran to his car and headed for the base.

CHAPTER 7

"Damn him, and the police. They may think I'll give up, but now I'm more determined to succeed. Once the twins are gone, I can start my life over with no fears. I'll be free. I'll find a way around their protectors and make the police look more inept than they already do."

"You're late," Bear frowned as Shadow rushed to join the other team members on the beach.

"I have a good reason."

"Tell me later. We're going to run up and down the beach along the water's edge. I don't want any of you going soft on me."

The others laughed and ran off. "Shadow, wait a moment. Run with me and tell me what happened."

Sun beat down on their heads and running on the soft sand took more effort, but Shadow managed to explain the incident with Anais.

"Then your instincts were right. Damn, I don't know how you do it."

"I don't even understand it. My mother said there are a few babies born who have the gift. My grandfather had it, it skipped my mother and her siblings, and then I was born with the gift. "

"If I hadn't seen how it works for you, I'd never have believed it. Hurry up. The guys are too far ahead." Bear sped up, and Shadow laughed, easily running to catch him and then past.

This type of exercise he could do without thinking about it. Instead, his head was full of thoughts about Anais. No matter how he tried to convince himself she wasn't so important to him, something happened to prove him wrong. He'd wanted to feel himself inside her warm tightness and being interrupted left him aching for completion. But he didn't have sex casually, never had. Making love to her was more serious than all the rest. He almost hoped for a mission. Time away to cool his hormones and clear his mind. He caught up with the others a few long strides before Bear.

"Going soft, Bear," Gordy teased.

"Do twenty push-ups, smart guy."

Gordy's teammates taunted him and then, starting with Heath, they all joined in and did the same number of push-ups.

"That's what I like to see," Bear said. "Any day now we may be called up for another mission. We need to be strong and a tight group." He glanced at Shadow. "You'll need to make plans for the twins while we're gone. Unless we catch this guy in the next few days."

"Yes, Sir."

"All right, we'll go get the boats and do more maneuvers."

During their break after the boat maneuvers, Bear joined Shadow and Heath where they sat at the outside picnic table. "If you want to eat, it's time to join the group headed to the mess hall."

"I need to talk with you," Shadow said. "Heath, I'll grab a bite later."

Heath nodded and walked toward his car.

"First, I have something to tell you," Bear said. "The captain contacted Tex and gave him a general idea of what had happened to Anais and Anya. Tex agreed to help, if necessary. Call him and bring him up to date on what's happened in regards to the twins. We may have to leave on a moment's notice."

"You seem certain it won't be long."

"The negotiations aren't doing well, as we expected. I give it at the most a week before we're called out."

"Then I'd like to put in for vacation."

"You're that serious about this lady?"

"Yes, Sir. I hate not to go with the team, but..."

"You'd never forgive yourself if something happens to her."

"Right."

"How long?"

"Two weeks."

"I'll ask Paul if his team can send a member to fill in for the two weeks," Bear said. "I'll get back to you. You will join us after two weeks."

"I understand, and thank you."

"Thank Paul. If he doesn't agree, you have to go. I'll ask Wolf to see if his friend can visit that little town and get more recent information."

Shadow nodded and headed to the chow hall to join Heath and the others.

"Have them come and stay with Cheryl. She's not

as busy in her new job, and even with Zane, she gets lonely at times."

"No. That might place Cheryl in danger."

"I thought we'd ask the captain to let them all stay on base in one of the houses like Cheryl did when she was in danger."

"Good idea. Does Zane like other dogs?"

"Most of them. Why?"

"I have a dog on the reservation. I left him with my mother. She's doing much better now, and I'm certain she wouldn't mind lending him to the twins temporarily."

"Have her bring him, and we'll see how they get along. What's his name?"

"Scout. He's old, but he's still strong. Now that I have a house, I'd been planning to get him, but he and Mom are close, so I hesitated."

"I like this plan. I'll talk with Cheryl tonight and see what she has to say."

"I won't mention it to the twins until I hear from you."

"He tried to attack you?" Anya asked, straightening up from the reclined hospital bed.

"Yes. If Shadow hadn't sneaked inside and hidden under the bed, I'd have had to shoot him, and aim to do serious injury. If that had happened, it would be my word against his."

"They would have believed you."

"I think so, but I'm glad Shadow was there."

"What was he doing under your bed?" Anya's smirk said she knew.

Anais laughed. "I'll let you figure that one out."

"I'm glad he cares about you. I haven't seen you smile so much since we had to leave home. But ..."

"I know. He's a SEAL, and this could end up hurting me." Anais shrugged. "I don't care. He makes me happy. I feel fully alive with him and safe."

"As long as you know the risk."

"I have lots of risks, but none of the others are fun and sexy." Both sisters laughed.

Anya's door opened and Dr. Andrews walked in. "Let me check your head." He touched the area where the bullet hit. "Does this hurt?"

"No, I have had a few headaches."

"You can expect them for a short time. All your vitals are good and your blood work. Are you ready to go home?"

"Yes, please."

"Okay. I want to see you in my office in a week for

a followup. The nurse will give you my address and the date and time before you leave." He gave Anya a stern stare. "I suspect you are very active. My directions, not suggestions, are to be lazy. Lay around, no exercises or exertion that might bring on a headache. Otherwise, I'll keep you in longer."

"I thought you said my brain is all right."

"It is, but your scalp has a fairly deep crease in it. You will get headaches if you don't behave. And let your sister lean down if you need to pick something up."

Anya glared at her doctor. "I think you're babying me."

"Perhaps, is that so terrible? I want to be sure my patients recover in a timely manner."

"Hmm, I'm not going to be a model patient." Anya said.

"I suspected you were the type to not follow directions."

"I don't see a ring on your finger. You haven't found a woman to put up with you. You must be as demanding at home. Are you a perfectionist or have some other weird habits?"

He leaned over laughing. When he caught his breath, he said, "No annoying habits that I know of, but I might be wrong. I've been busy doctoring and having fun. I like sports, mountain climbing, and such."

"Mountain climbing. Now there is a sport I wouldn't try."

"Why, because you don't like heights?"

"I don't like being cold."

"It's a great sport."

Anya glanced at Anais, who was holding back her laughter.

Dr. Andrews waved and added, "See you next week at my office."

"If I'm still alive," she mumbled as he disappeared.

Anais burst out laughing. "I think you've met your match. It's obvious he likes you, and you like him."

"No, I love to tease."

"Yes, you are attracted to him. He's good-looking, and I think he might understand how to manage you."

"I'm not manageable."

"We'll see. I'll get your dirty clothes out of the closet. Here are clean ones I brought from home."

WHEN SHADOW GOT OFF WORK, HE HEADED HOME AND called his mother. "Hi, Mom."

"How are you? Something must be up, since I'm getting two calls so close together."

"I'll try and do better when I'm in port."

"Do. I love hearing your voice."

"Mom, would you be upset if I brought Scout to San Diego, at least for a while?"

"I'll miss him, but your Uncle Fred's Lab had puppies, and I might take one. Scout has been company for me. It doesn't look as though you are going to give me any grandchildren anytime soon."

"I will, be patient."

"Well, you must like this lady. You've never given me any hope before."

"I do like her."

"Good. I'll bring Scout to you. I want to meet her."

"I'll arrange a place on the base for you."

"Why can't I stay at your house?"

"Because my lady and her sister are in danger, and they may be living on the base or with me. I don't want any of their problems to become yours."

"All right. I'll pack up tonight and start driving in your direction tomorrow."

"It's a long drive for you alone."

"I can't fly Scout on a plane. He'd hate it and might cause trouble."

"Have one of your brothers drive you."

"They're all busy with their businesses. I'll be fine. Don't come. You worry too much."

"I don't care. You are invaluable to me."

"That's the sweetest thing you've ever said."

Shadow heard her sniff. "Please don't cry."

"It's happy tears."

"I'll call you back in a few hours. Captain Buchanan is considering giving me some leave time. If he does, I'll get you here."

"Bring the lady who has spiked your interest. She can ride back with us."

"I doubt she'd want that long turnaround trip. Talk to you soon, Mom."

Shadow called Bear. "Any word from Paul?"

"He got right back to me. He has a guy who will fill in for the two weeks. You may have to pay it back when he goes on vacation in a few months."

"No problem. Hopefully, by that time, this will be over and the twins safe. I've asked my mother to come and bring Scout. I'll have to fly there overnight and drive her back. I don't want her making the trip on her own. She's able to do it, but there's weird, bad people traveling who might spot she's alone."

"Scout would scare most of them off. But I wouldn't let my mother drive that far alone either. Wait a moment. I have an idea. I'll check and call you right back."

"Okay." Shadow put his cell away and shrugged. He headed to the kitchen and made a bacon, lettuce and tomato sandwich, and then took that, chips, and a glass of lemonade out to his table near the pool.

His cell rang as he swallowed the first bite of his sandwich. "That was quick."

"I called Commander Walsh. He's a good guy, and we talk frequently. He's visiting his brother in Montana and he's heading back in two days. Your Mom's not too far from where he's staying. He'll swing by and pick her and Scout up. He said they'd take a break at night, so they'll arrive in about four days."

"Wow. You're sure he won't mind?"

"No, he says he hates the drive alone. He lost his wife about three years ago from cancer. He could fly, but he likes the scenery, just not the emptiness of the car. He's mentioned it before, so I knew he'd be happy to have company coming home. Will your Mom feel all right traveling with a stranger?"

"A navy officer isn't a stranger to my Mother. But

tell him not to try anything. She has a concealed weapon with her at all times."

Bear laughed. "I'll warn the Commander. He'll get a good laugh out of that."

"I'll call Mom, and tell her the plans."

"Let me know if she feels the least bit uncomfortable about it. Then you'll have to fly and get her."

"Thanks again, Bear. I'll talk to her and call you back either way."

"Good. Enjoy your time off and be careful. I don't want to lose a team member at all, but especially stateside."

"You guys be safe."

"Always." Bear clicked off.

Shadow immediately called his mother and told her the plans. "Are you all right riding with him? He is a stranger."

"No, he's not. I think I met him when I was at Coronado visiting your Dad. He was Team Four's leader at the time. I liked him. He was smart, witty, and he and his wife were very nice. I'm sorry he lost her. We'll be fine. I look forward to having his company on the trip."

"He'll be coming to get you in two days. I'll call Bear back and give him your number so

Commander Walsh can reach you and get directions."

"Good. See you soon, Kijika."

After clicking off, Shadow called Bear.

"She's looking forward to seeing him. They met years ago, and he made a good impression on her. My mother wants him to have her number so she can give him the best directions to get to her house."

"Sounds like they'll have a good trip. I wonder if the commander remembers her."

"I wish Scout could talk. I'd like to get a report on that trip," Shadow said and laughed. "Thanks for everything Bear."

"That's what I'm here for, to keep my men happy."

Shadow considered calling Anais, but decided to call the hospital. The operator rang Anya's room. No one answered. He checked with the operator and learned Anya was discharged earlier in the day.

I'm glad I checked, now I can go straight to their house. Shadow packed a few changes of clothes and headed to the garage. *I have two weeks to solve two mysteries—catch whoever's after the twins, and find out if Anais and I are right for each other.*

❄

THE POLICE OFFICER ON GUARD DUTY OPENED THE front door and carried in the small bag with Anya's dirty clothes. After he put the bag down, he checked the house before going out front.

"It seems strange to have police around," Anya said.

"I know. Shadow called in and told them he'd be late getting here. The Chief said his guy would leave whenever Shadow arrives."

"You're falling love with him."

"What makes you think so?"

"Anais, we're twins and closer than regular sisters. I see how you look at him, and I feel your desire to have a relationship rather than just having him here to keep us safe."

"I do want more, but he's never going to trust me after all that's happened."

"I have faith he'll look past all the weird happenings in our lives right now and see the real you."

"We'll see. I guess this will be another day of waiting for this guy to strike. Nothing is going to happen while we're so closely guarded," Anais said.

"Are you suggesting we draw him out so they can capture him?"

"Better than dying of boredom."

"Thank you, but I'd rather not die at all. I'm going to my room to change into shorts."

Anais had sat down in the living room and was reading the paper when there was a knock at the door. She jumped before she heard Shadow's voice. First, she checked before opening the door, as he'd instructed them. "You scared me. I thought someone had knocked off our cop."

"No, he's right here. He won't leave until you say it's all right."

"You can leave, Officer. My warrior friend will keep us safe, but thanks for taking care of us."

"No problem." He shook Shadow's hand. "That's quite a handle she gave you. I wish my girlfriend would give me one like it." He waved and got in his car to drive off.

"Nice guy, not like that first creep."

"I'm surprised you didn't have to go to work."

Shadow pulled her close to him. "I took a two-week vacation." He leaned down and kissed her.

"Why? I hate for you to have to use your time off keeping us safe. You probably would rather visit your mother."

"She's coming here and will arrive in three or four days."

"Then you won't be guarding us."

"Yes, I will. I was going to have you two stay on base, but since I got my vacation, Mom can stay at my house and so can you and your sister. I have plenty of room. Maybe you'd agree to share mine."

"Not with your mom there. She'd think I was awful."

"I doubt that, but I understand." He kissed her. "I'm aching to finish what we started the other night."

"Me, too. When the time is right."

"Yes, my dear."

"So that's why you were so handily in Anais's room when the officer tried to attack my sister." Anya had entered the room and heard the end of their conversation.

"You suspected," Anais said.

"Yes, I did." Anya smiled at Shadow. "I'm glad. You're a good man. I haven't said that to every guy she's dated."

Anais grinned. "No, she's usually finding fault with them. What she told you is high praise from my sister."

"Thanks, Anya. Let's get you two moved into my house today. Then we'll be all settled in when Mom arrives."

"I suppose this is necessary," Anya said.

"Yes."

"I'll go pack my suitcase for our visit to your house."

Shadow looked puzzled, and Anais laughed.

"My sister loves to catch people off guard. It means she likes you."

"Good to know. Go pack. I'll check around the house and make certain it's locked up tight."

"It is, the police officer went through it earlier. But I know SEALs don't think anyone can do it better than them."

Shadow wriggled his eyebrows. "No one can."

"I think you are not referring to the house."

"You're right." He pushed her forward down the hall. "Hurry, let's get out of here."

CHAPTER 8

SHADOW SHOWED THE TWINS THEIR ROOMS AND LEFT them unpacking. Of course, he put Anais right next to his bedroom. His cell rang as he walked down the hall.

"Hi, Bear."

"I've been thinking. We'll be headed out, but I talked to Paul about sending one of his men down to the Keys where this guy told his wife he had gone. I know from the way you've been acting you don't quite believe this man is the person in San Diego.

"I didn't have Ranger and Hawke check the Keys. I wanted them back here in case the mission we were waiting on came up quickly, which it has.

"I know your instincts are seldom wrong, but I think they may be this time. Anyway, Paul said he'd like a little vacation before they go out on another mission. He's flying to Miami today and will take the picture with him."

"That's great. But I have a feeling we've headed down a rabbit hole."

"Paul will be in touch with you. I'll be out of range for a while. Keep Captain Buchanan updated."

"Will do and thanks."

"Just get this done."

"I intend too." Shadow headed into his kitchen to check on food. With all the company, he'd need to add to his groceries.

"Worrying about feeding us?" Anya asked.

"I don't keep much food on hand."

"Typical guy. I'll check with you and Anais, and I will plan the meals for the next few days. Your Mother might rather do more shopping when she arrives."

"True. Thanks for the help. I'll drive you two to the grocery store. Let me know when you're ready. "

"And you two do whatever you want until your Mom arrives." Anya grinned. "I won't be checking any bedrooms before I go to sleep and I'm a sound sleeper."

"Thanks for the heads up, but I'll see how Anais feels about it."

"Are there any more around like you?"

"Maybe your doctor. I liked him. Anais said you two were flirting."

"Perhaps, a little."

Anais joined them. "You have a lovely house, Shadow. Hope you don't mind that I peeked around a little on my way to the kitchen. I heard your voices, so I followed the sound. Do you swim much in the pool?"

"Some at night. If you two want to swim, I'll join you or sit at the table and watch."

"I'll feel less claustrophobic if I can spend time outdoors," Anais said.

"I'm glad I have the pool."

"I've started a list for groceries. Add whatever you want," Anya handed her sister the sheet. "I barely got started."

Shadow stood back and watched the two. Surprisingly, it was fun. One would start to add something to the list at the same time the other mentioned it. They'd laugh and go on searching his pantry and coming up with more food ideas.

Anya looked around. "I love your pantry. It's huge compared to most. Ours is about half the size."

"I don't need one this big, but I've wanted a house in this area for a long time. When this one came up for sale, I was in port. I called the first day and sealed the deal."

"Why were you so eager?" Anais asked.

"I hated living in a condo, and several of my friends live on this street and two streets over."

"We considered a condo, but Anais wanted more space and to live in a neighborhood. If we ever lived apart, I'd go for a condo. I like big houses, but I hate the time it would take to keep one clean."

"At work, they teach us to keep our equipment in shape and clean. For most of us, it spills over into keeping our home orderly and clean. There's a few we tease about being slobs, but not many."

"I can see they won't call you a slob," Anais said.

"No, and my mother is the reason for part of that training. She said boys needed to keep a house as well as a woman, and even if married, housekeeping was not just a woman's job."

"Did your Dad help around the house?" Anya asked.

"When he was home or Mom would give him the evil eye."

"Then we'd better make certain your house is very neat and clean when she arrives." Anais showed him their completed list.

"Looks good. Who's going to cook?" Shadow asked.

"We both will. Anya likes it the least, but she does her share."

"Let's get to the store and back. I'll check around outside before we leave, then I'll take you one by one to the truck."

"You think this person knows already where we are living?" Anya frowned. "I doubt he's that smart."

"I hope you're right, but we aren't taking a chance. I didn't see a similar car following us, and we'll do shopping in this area."

"Fine."

"DAMN, DAMN, DAMN!" IT SEEMED THAT RENTING A different make and model of car has been a useless expense. Because some fucking guy didn't keep going through the yellow light, and the twins sailed on through the intersection. Now I must backtrack and wait for them to return from wherever they'd gone. "I want this ended, now. I have a life and I want to live it."

Paul arrived in Miami in the early afternoon. He rented a car and decided to start the drive toward Key West. He'd stop overnight at various towns and check for this guy. The picture looked like an average joe about forty years old, not the type to stand out in a crowd.

Once on his way, he put down the windows and enjoyed the breeze and salt air smell. When he stopped, he rented a room near the highway and asked where he'd find a restaurant with a bar. The young man behind the counter showed him a map of the area and marked an X over The Lobster House. "The visitors seem to like it best, but if you want the place the locals prefer, it's Buster's Shanty Shack. Most of it's in the open. Part of the seats for eating are around the bar. There's a small eating area inside."

"I like the sound of the place."

"Then walk two blocks down, turn left and go down three blocks. "You'll hear the music before you arrive."

Paul changed into a casual shirt and shorts, then enjoyed the walk. The music greeted him a block before he arrived. There was one empty spot at the bar. The guy in the seat beside Paul's greeted him.

"I can see you're a stranger to these parts. You

don't have our local accent, and you look like a tourist. But we're glad to have you visit. Welcome. I'm Henry. If you plan to order food, try the shrimp sandwich and fries. It's the best."

"Thanks. I take it you're a local."

"Born and raised here. I don't need to go to the mainland. It's full of crazy people stepping all over folks to get rich."

"You describe it pretty well." Paul took a drink of his beer and ordered what Henry suggested.

"What's a guy like you doing here? Clean-cut, personable. Not our type."

"I don't know. I'm going to check all the Keys. I may retire here after I leave the Navy. Here's question for you. A friend of mine came to the Keys a while back. He called his wife and said he planned to stay, but didn't mention where he'd settle. His wife was worried. Since I had a vacation to Florida planned, she wanted me to check on him."

"He settled here without his wife?"

Paul shrugged. "Let's just say he's a bit of a unique individual."

"Then he should fit right in down here. You got a picture?"

"Sure do." Paul pulled out the grainy copy. "It's

not too good. I didn't go by her house. I live about fifty miles away."

"Are you two good friends? I'd expect you'd have several pictures of the two of you fishing or doing somethin'." Henry squinted at Paul. "You're the cops or in some similar job, maybe a private eye."

"True, the wife hired me long distance. I got the picture from their local paper."

"Thought so. Do you think this guy left his wife for good?"

"Said he wanted a divorce."

"Yeah, we see some like that. The husband can't face the wife, and so they head this way. Many of them stay." He chuckled. "One wife came all this way and found her husband here. She hit him with everything available and then hauled him off to her car. We had a good laugh, but I often wondered if he made it home alive."

"Did he look like this?"

Henry held the picture up to better see it.

"Nope, no one lookin' like him has been here."

"Thanks, Henry. By the way, my name's, Paul. I'm going to eat this delicious-looking sandwich and go back to my motel. I'll leave early in the morning to continue my search. But one day, I'm going to surprise you and come back for another beer and sandwich."

Henry slapped him on the back. "I'll be lookin' for you. Plan on staying longer next time. I'd better get home, or my lady will be chasing me there."

Paul laughed. He ate and stayed longer, showing the picture to the waitress and bartender. But they were as certain as Henry had been. No one recognized the man.

The next morning he headed to the next town. *Maybe I'll be luckier today.*

THE TWINS WATCHED WHILE SHADOW STARTED A FIRE in the fireplace. Then they all sat and talked about everything, but the danger that surrounded them.

Anya finished her drink and got up and stretched. "I'm tired. Hospitals aren't the place to get any rest. You two have fun," she said and winked.

"Is she going to bed early to give us alone time?" Shadow asked as he moved over and sat on the sofa beside Anais.

"A bit of both. I can tell Anya is tired. I suspect she may still be having headaches. I'm glad we'll have time alone before your Mother arrives." She reached out for him, and he pulled her into his arms. "I feel safe when you hug me," Anais said.

Shadow slid his hand over her auburn hair, and then tipped her chin up. "Everything about you is soft, and you smell like fresh air and sunshine."

Anais chuckled. "Anya keeps telling me to buy sexier perfume."

"Don't change it. I like the fragrance. Women who wear heavy perfume turn me off."

"Good to know."

Shadow leaned down and kissed her. "I'd like to carry you to my room and continue where we left off at your house."

"Show me the way."

He picked her up and walked to the end of the hall. "This house was built a bit differently. The master suite is at the end and quite large." He kicked the door open and dropped her on his bed. "Just where I want you." He lay down beside her.

"I don't want to rush you, so tell me to slow down if I'm moving too fast."

Anais put her hand against his cheek. "When you looked at me that first night, my heart jumped. I wanted to reach out and touch you, but I had no idea if you were a good guy or bad."

"It was the same for me. But I was in deep and

couldn't say much. I just knew I wanted to make sure you got home safe. But let's not talk. Let me show you how I feel." He pulled her short top off, exposing her breasts. He kissed each pert nipple and felt her quiver. "Are you frightened?"

"No, my body is hungry for your touch. It's a reaction from our long period of anticipation. Don't stop."

He lay on top of her body and kissed her face, her forehead, each eyelid, and the corner of her mouth. When he looked into her eyes, a sensuous light passed between them. He kissed her hard, and her lips opened, hungry for more. His tongue swirled around inside tasting her sweetness. He bit teasingly at her lip. There seemed to be a sense of urgency after their prolonged delay.

When he kissed her neck and felt the rapid beating of her pulse, he looked up. His gaze traveled over her face and stopped when he looked into her eyes.

"You want me as much as I want you." It wasn't a question, but she nodded anyway.

"We'll go slow and savor the touch and taste of each other." He slid down and cupped her breasts in his hands. His fingers rubbed across the tips, and her body rose up against his. Moving down slower, he kissed her flat abdomen and smelled her womanly essence.

"I'm not sure I can go as slow as I want to. I want you now. I'm aching to touch you intimately."

"I feel the same. Make me yours."

Shadow rose up and pulled her underwear and shorts off. Then he stepped off the bed to take his own clothes off and put on a condom.

When he put his knee on the bed, he stopped for a second and asked, "You're sure? I can't make any promises at this time. We still have so much learning to do about each other."

"I'm sure. Stop talking and make love to me. We'll take it day by day."

He kissed and touched her body all the way down to her most intimate spot.

In a breathless tone, she whispered, "Hurry."

He gazed at her and his expression sent a tremor throughout her body. "Who's in a rush? I want to enjoy your sweetness and beauty from top to bottom."

THEN SHADOW PROCEEDED TO FILL HER WITH JOY AND her body arched to get closer and closer. Deep inside, her blood raced through her veins. A deep feeling of joy spread throughout her body when he held her tight against him and they found their release.

Shadow lay beside her and pulled her against his side. "Are you all right? I was so hungry for you that I treated you less gently than I'd planned."

"You were magnificent, and I didn't want gentle. I wanted all of you. You must have noticed I enjoyed all of our lovemaking."

He brushed her damp hair off her forehead. "Let's shower and sleep for a little while. But I plan to wake you at dawn and make love to every inch of you."

I won't be able to sleep with the anticipation you've aroused."

"You'll sleep."

LATER, AFTER THEIR SHOWER, THEY LAY WITH THEIR bodies curved into each other. Shadow's hand rested beside her breast, and he felt Anais's heartbeat under his hand. She'd gone to sleep shortly after they'd returned to bed and made love one more time.

Shadow lay awake. He wondered how this woman he cuddled so close would change his life. She was loving, intelligent, and beautiful. It was difficult to imagine how he'd say good-bye if this didn't work out between them.

One thing he was certain about, the person trying to kill her and her sister was not going to succeed. More and more, he suspected the person they thought was after them was nowhere around. So, who else might be angry enough to want them dead?

I have to find out before I run out of time.

ANAIS SLIPPED OUT OF BED AND GRABBED HER clothes. She got to the door before Shadow spoke.

"Did you think you might slip out without me knowing?" He sat up, and the covers fell to his waist.

Her heart raced when she looked at his broad chest. He was all tanned skin and muscles. She hesitated. She wanted to rush back to him, but feared she'd lose her heart when he went off on his own.

His gaze slid down from her mouth and stopped at her breasts. Her nipples peaked in reaction. She yanked her gown up in front of her and rushed out of his room to hers. After showering, she put on a modest blouse and jeans.

Shadow laughed when she came into the kitchen. "No shorts today? It's going to be warm." He moved closer and whispered in her ear. "You can't erase the vision I have of you in my mind."

Anya, seated at the table with a cup of coffee, gave him a sly smile. "I see my sister is blushing. You must be whispering sweet things in her ear."

"Anya, stop." Anais felt the heat in her face and knew if she looked, her skin would be bright red. Her sweet sister never had that problem, as nothing seemed to embarrass her.

"I hope you two slept well," Anya said. "I did. Your guest room is very comfortable."

"Anya, why don't you and Shadow go outside and sit. I'll fix breakfast and bring it to you."

"It sounds like a good idea to me. Are you joining me, Shadow?"

"In a minute. I want to speak with Anais about something." After Anya walked out, Shadow took Anais's hand and pulled her over to the table and down to sit on his lap. "Did I upset you in some way last night? This morning you've been shy and kept a distance between us." He smiled. "I love your blushes."

"Anya's lucky. I haven't seen anything yet make her blush."

"You're avoiding my question."

"You did nothing wrong. It was all too perfect."

"And how is that bad?"

"I'm afraid I'll come to care too much. I have a feeling you're comfortable with your life as it is. It's fun to play around and have sex, but what happens when you return from your next mission?"

Shadow cocked his head to the side. "We keep getting to know each other?"

Anais bit the side of her lip and stared at him.

"I can't promise forever right now. We have to find this person trying to kill you two. I have to join my team in two weeks. Too much is happening for me to know the future."

She jumped off his lap. "You're right, and I can't throw my heart out there to get hurt. I'll sleep in my room from now on."

He stood and gave her a long look. "Sometimes we have to put ourselves out there and risk it all."

"That goes both ways."

"Yes, it does." He bent and brushed his lips across hers. "I'll join your sister."

Anais understood the phase, "your heart breaks," and wondered if she had the strength to risk it all. *Anya never backs down. It's time I acted more like her.*

AFTER TWO MORE DAYS OF STRIKING OUT, PAUL GOT weary. *I think this is a wild goose chase.* There were simply too many small islands markers along the way where a person could hide. *I'm almost to Marathon. I'll stop at the next gas station and call Shadow, since Bear's off on a mission.*

"Hi, Paul. Did you find this guy?"

"Not a trace and did you know the number of key markers there are along this route? I'm not far from Key West. I'll check it out after Marathon. But if this guy wants to hide, this is the place to go. It'd take much longer than I want to use of my vacation time to check this area completely. I'm going to return to Miami after Key West."

"That's fine. I appreciate the work you've done."

"It's an interesting place. I may visit a couple of the Keys again. How about I fly from Miami to Raleigh, North Carolina? You can send me the directions from there to the twins' hometown. I'll rent another car and check the place out. Maybe the guy decided to return home to his wife after all."

"I doubt it, but if you want to check the area again, that's fine."

"I heard a funny story about a wife driving to the Keys, finding her husband, beating him up and dragging him back home. Maybe this wife did the same."

"I doubt it. Do me a favor and visit the wife. See if she'll talk with you."

"No problem. I'll be in touch."

CHAPTER 9

"ANY NEWS?" ANYA ASKED WHEN SHADOW PUT UP his cell.

"None. My friend hasn't found any evidence your councilman went to the Keys. But he said there's a large number of islands along the drive to Key West. After checking there, he's going to fly to North Carolina and visit your hometown."

"What do you think he'll find that the other SEAL didn't?

"Nothing, probably. But my neck's tingling and has been for a while. I don't think we have the right information."

"Well, no one's been around for days," Anya said. "I intend to get out of here soon and do something."

"I'll be following behind."

"Darn."

Shadow and Anais shared a smile as Anya stomped off to her room. Anais said, "She thinks she can take care of herself and even a shot in the head hasn't convinced her otherwise."

"Or getting kidnapped," Shadow added.

"I think the bravado may be a cover to hide the fear she won't admit."

"I'd ask you to play with me in my room," Shadow said. "But I expect my mother to call at any moment and say they're close."

His cell rang with a different tone just as he spoke. "I swear my Mom has a special link to me."

He grinned and answered. "Hi."

"We're almost to your door. I didn't want to pop in without calling first when you have such lovely company."

"Mom." Shadow felt his cheeks turning red.

She laughed. "I love to tease you, Kijika. You are too serious most of the time. See you soon." Shadow glanced around and saw the twins in full swing cleaning the room, which wasn't messy.

"My mother isn't going to judge you by the cleanliness of my house. She knows my house is seldom messy."

"And so if it is, she'll know we made the mess."

Anais stood with her hands on her hips. "Don't bother us. We have to check our rooms."

Shadow grinned as they rushed off. *Mom's going to like them, especially Anais.*

Anais and Anya came back dressed in nicer clothes, and they'd added makeup. Shadow raised an eyebrow. "All this for my mother?"

"Yes. We want to make a good first impression."

All three looked toward the front of the house as the doorbell sounded. "You're just in time," Shadow said.

He opened the door and reached for his Mother. He hugged her and spun her around.

"Put me down. I'm getting too old to be flung in the air. But don't stop the hugs."

She patted his cheek, and he blushed again.

A dog pushed past her legs to throw himself against Shadow. "You missed me, Scout." Shadow ran his hands through Scout's thick golden hair. "How did he travel?"

"Fine, but I have someone else I want you to meet.

I think you know Larry. I mean, Commander Walsh."

"Yes, we've met a few times. Welcome to my home. Please come in."

He turned to see Anais coming from the kitchen. "My sister and I thought you might be thirsty from your trip. I hope you like iced tea. We made it last night. Anya will bring the snacks in a moment."

"Anais, I'd like you to meet my mother, Rozene, my family calls her Rose, and Commander Walsh. And I'd like you to meet Anais Kenly. Her sister is Anya. Shall we go out into the garden and enjoy our drinks and snacks?"

Scout ran ahead of them.

"What a beautiful Labrador. I've haven't seen many yellow ones."

"I'm surprised. Yellow labs are very popular. Mom brought him back to me. He's been staying with her. He's a good scout. That's how he got his name. I wanted help keeping an eye on you two," Shadow said and rubbed the top of Scout's head.

Shadow followed behind them. He didn't miss the smile his mother gave the commander or the fact they joined hands on the way outside.

He grabbed another chair from around the pool and put it by the table. His mother and Anais had already sat with the commander. Anais started to explain why she and Anya were staying with Shadow. Shadow almost groaned.

Commander Walsh isn't in charge of my team, but he

might let our team's commander know how much we're embroiled at the present time. Captain Buchanan talked with our commander, but things may change if Commander Walsh talks with him.

Anya joined them with a tray of snacks, pulled up another chair and sat by her sister. Shadow sat in the empty seat by Commander Walsh.

"This is a lovely treat. I'm fascinated by how much you look alike," Shadow's Mom said.

Anya glanced at Shadow. "He can tell us apart easily. Since he met us, he's had no difficulty knowing which of us was Anais."

"Ah, your personalities must be different," Shadow's mom said.

Anais agreed. "My sister is the more outgoing one, and I'm more reserved."

"What do you each do for a living?" the commander asked.

Anya spoke up. "I'm a psychologist. That's what got us into danger. My sister is an internist. But I'll let her tell you about herself."

"Thanks Anya. I loved being a doctor, but while we're here I decided to not apply for my license. I'll wait and see if we want to stay in California. For now, I've taken up painting and volunteering at one of the hospitals."

"Kenly?" Shadow's mother looked at Anais. "Your mother must be the famous artist, Dacey Kenly. Now that I know the connection, I see how much you both look like her."

"You're not the first person this week to recognize her name. Wait until I tell Mom. She's very modest about her work."

"I met her once at a showing in New York. I was also doing a showing of my Native American jewelry in another room. We met and talked briefly.

"When Kijika' introduced you two, I knew you reminded me of someone. She impressed me with her sweetness. She was not a snobbish type of celebrity."

"Mom said she'd never go to a big city again. She prefers being home with her work," Anais said.

"I'd like to see some of your paintings. I suspect you're very good and don't want to admit it."

"Nothing like my mother," Anais said. "Do you still design your jewelry?"

"I didn't for several years. I do it more as a hobby now."

"I haven't seen her work yet," Commander Walsh said. "I'm going to encourage her to do more now that I've heard she had a show in New York. But only if she wants to." He turned to Shadow. "What's the latest on the hunt for the man trying to kill these nice young ladies?"

"I think whoever is after Anais and Anya didn't manage to follow us to my house. There's been no hint of anyone sneaking around."

"You say 'whoever' and 'anyone' instead of guy or man? Is there a reason for vague descriptors?"

"Maybe. I'd had some crazy thoughts about this for some time." For a few minutes, they drank the tea and ate the snacks. After they'd finished eating, Shadow's mother put her hand on the commander's arm and spoke up.

"I've decided to stay with Larry at his house. We want to get to know each other better, and I'm sure your lady friends will be more comfortable without your mother around every minute." She held up her hand when Shadow started to speak. "Let me finish. We'll visit often, but will call first. If you need Larry for any advice or help..." She smiled up at him. "He has assured me he'd be glad to be of assistance."

"But Mom, you always stay with me."

"True, but this is different circumstances. I want to have more time with Larry."

Commander Walsh grinned and patted her hand. "I think your son would prefer you to call me Commander Walsh, my dear."

"Don't be silly. We're old enough to do as we want, and I'm very sure my son wants to see me happy."

Stunned, Shadow looked from his mother's smiling face to the commander's. "But you've never shown any interest in another man since Dad died."

"My dear, I may be your mother and fifty-six years old, but I am still a vital woman. You do want me to be happy, don't you?"

Damn, there goes my blush. He hadn't blushed this must since junior high. It was clear his mother and the others were waiting for him to say something.

"I'm surprised, but I do want you to be happy, and Commander Walsh is a fine man."

"I'm proud of you. I knew you'd understand. Now, we're going to Larry's house to unpack. Shall we have dinner out or is that too dangerous?"

"I vote for dining out," Anya said. "We'll never get this over with if we don't show ourselves."

"It's dangerous," Shadow said.

"Anais and I can't continue to live this way. We want our lives back."

Before Shadow could answer, the commander spoke. "She's right. We'll lessen the risk. I'll ask for some of our men in regular clothes to be outside and inside the restaurant. They won't raise any suspicions, and these two ladies will be safe."

"All right, if Anais and Anya agree."

Anais hugged Shadow's arm. "Please let us do this. I so want to be a doctor again"—she smiled into his eyes—"before I forget what I know."

"All right, but I'd like to talk privately with Commander Walsh about how we'll be handling your security."

His mother stood and, arm-in-arm, walked inside with the twins. Scout followed them. Shadow heard his mom say how she wanted to get to know them better.

"I'm sure your mother has surprised you, and I want to reassure you that I sincerely care about her. I know this is quick, but you can learn much about a person while traveling together. We're not sure where this is going, but we want to give it a chance.

I do want the two of you to be happy. It's been quite a surprise to me. Just give me time to get used to the idea. Now, you'll want to know how we've been handling the twins' dangerous situation."

Shadow told the commander all they'd done and how Anya got shot, and Anais almost run down. "So we know this person is serious about killing them."

"You think this person isn't necessarily a man."

155

"I believe it may very well be a woman. I can't explain why, but nothing adds up. Paul is going back to the twins' hometown. I'm anxious to hear if he finds out anything."

"You need to let Paul know you suspect the killer may be female."

"I will. I'll call him after you all leave."

"Good. We'll pick you up later. We can go together, and the killer is less likely to know my SUV."

"Thank you, for your help and for taking such good care of my mother on the trip."

When they joined the ladies, Commander Walsh put his arm around Rose. "Let's go, dear, and get settled in my place before it's time for dinner."

Rose took hold of one of each of the twins' hands. "You are lovely ladies and made my visit so delightful. We'll look forward to seeing you tonight."

When Shadow closed the door and turned to the twins, Anya said, "Didn't you ever consider your mother might find someone else to love?"

"No, she seemed settled and happy."

"Well, there's content and then there's happy. You can be both, but for a woman, they aren't the same. Your mother is attractive and vibrant," Anais said.

"And the commander is good-looking for his age," Anya added.

"I don't want to discuss this right now." Shadow strode down the hall into a small room he'd turned into a study.

He was relieved they didn't follow him. He felt a little off balance. *It's silly of me, but I didn't ever consider my mother might remarry.* His cell phone rang and showed an unfamiliar number.

"Hello, this is Gibson speaking."

"This is Police Chief Edwards in Pensacola, Florida. A couple of your friends visited our town recently. One was a Mr. Dirk Foster. I heard his friend call him Ranger. He left his card with his number and yours. I haven't been able to reach him, so I'm calling you."

"He's out of town. How can I help you, Chief Edwards?"

"I don't know if you can, but one of our fishermen walked into a dense woods where he sometimes fishes. There's a small river that flows through, but most of the fishermen don't like the dense forest and thick bushes they have to walk through to get there. I'm trying to explain why no one found the dead body until now."

"I understand. How I can help?"

"Well, the medical examiner says the man has been dead a long time. But from what he came up with, the height and hair color match that of the man your friends were looking for when they came to Pensacola. The dead man's fingerprints aren't on file, and we haven't had anyone reported missing in our area. I thought Mr. Foster might get something with his friend's DNA on it and send it to us as soon as possible."

"I'll get you what you need right away. The local police where Mr. Foster's friend lived can go to the house and ask his wife for something of his."

"I'd think by now the wife would be worried and have the police searching for him."

"Supposedly, he called and told her he wanted a divorce."

"I wonder how she felt about him divorcing her?"

"I'd like to find out. I'll get back to you, Chief Edwards. Thanks for the call."

Shadow went to the door and called out for Anais and Anya.

"What's up?" Anya asked.

"I had quite an interesting phone call from Pensacola, Florida," Shadow repeated all the information Edwards had told him.

"You think it's my patient?"

"Might be. I want Anais to call the police chief in your hometown. Tell him what you found out. Ask him to contact the wife, get some personal item of her husband's, and the chief can send it to Pensacola."

"If it's him, then who's been shooting at us?" Anais asked.

"I'm not sure, but I have an idea. Make the call, talk real sweet to the chief, and then put me on."

"Hello, can I speak with the Chief Daly? I'm Anais Kenly. I have some information for him. Thanks, I'll hold." She handed the phone to Shadow.

"Hi, Chief Daly. This is Chief Petty Officer Gibson. I thought you wouldn't know my name, so I asked Anais to call. I'm a friend of the twins."

"Is this important and if so, what's it about?"

"Chief, this is very important. A friend of mine was there recently looking for a mutual friend. He also went to Pensacola and left his name and mine at the police station."

"Girard Steen?"

"Yes, your councilman. We've been looking for him. It seems they've found a body in thick woods near Pensacola and they don't have any locals missing. We thought of your man. Can you get a personal item from Mrs. Steen to send to Chief Edwards, in Pensacola?"

"I'm afraid not. Marian's visiting friends in Arizona."

"Do you have a number for these friends?"

"No, but I'll go to her house and get something of his and send it to Pensacola. I'll also look for her address book and get the address and number for her friends. Since we think the man is her husband and he's dead, I can use my authority to enter her home," Chief Daly said.

"Thanks, I appreciate the help." Shadow hung up the phone. His neck was tingling more than usual. *My theory is going to turn out to be right.* He glanced at the twins. "You heard my end of the conversation. What do you think?"

"It seems strange his wife would leave and go to Arizona. But maybe she couldn't live in the house or town after he threw her over," Anais said.

Shadow glanced at Anya. He knew from her expression she was on the same track as he was. The difference between the twins was showing now. Anais looked for the good, kind answer, but Anya was much more worldly and suspicious.

"He'll call me back." Shadow glanced at his

watch. "I know you ladies can take a long time getting ready. Maybe you'd like to start now."

"It doesn't take us that long," Anais protested. "I'm going to get my swimsuit and try out your pool."

"I'll be lazy and watch." *I intend to keep my clothes on and my cell close.*

He enjoyed watching the two swim. They were excellent swimmers and challenged each other in races up and down the pool. They won an equal amount. When his phone rang, Shadow headed toward his study. Scout stayed behind and lay by the pool. "Good boy, Scout."

Shadow answered the phone as he entered his study. "Gibson."

"This is Chief Daly. I went to the house, and it wasn't difficult to get inside. The house was messy, unusual for Marian. She always kept an impeccable house. I noticed some personal items, like a figurine missing, but she might have broke it or took it with her. From the looks of the house, I'm wondering if she plans to return. She took all of her clothes."

"Very interesting. Did you find her address book?"

"No, she must have it. But she saved a lot of her mail over the years. I found a box full of cards and personal letters in the bedroom closet, several of them with an Arizona name and address. I looked it up and found the phone number online."

He gave the number to Shadow.

"It's difficult to believe my councilman is dead, but I sent a shirt and both toothbrushes special delivery to Edwards. Maybe we'll soon find out what happened."

"Thanks for all your work and help. I'll keep you up-to-date from this end."

"Do, and thanks for getting in touch. By the way tell Anya I fired the detective she talked with about her concerns regarding our councilman. My detective didn't believe what she told him about his friend. He never mentioned the talk he had with Anya to me until recently."

"I'll let her know. And thanks, I couldn't have done all you did, so quickly and thoroughly."

Shadow disconnected the call.

"Now that you've thanked everyone, tell us what's up," Anya said impatiently. They'd showered and dressed then stepped inside his office to hear the last few words.

"I have the wife's friend's number in Arizona, but I'm going to wait until I have the results of the DNA testing before calling her friend. If it takes too long, I'll go ahead and get in touch with her."

Anais squinted her eyes and studied him. "You've suspected all along it was a woman after us, haven't you."

"What?" Anya looked at her sister like she'd lost her mind.

"Why else did the person wear a big hood over their head, if not to fool us of their gender? I fear the next attack will be fierce," Anais said. "She must be getting impatient."

Shadow stared at her. "You'd make a good detective."

Anya shook her head. "I'm surprised I didn't figure it out. Wow, I'm proud of you, Anais."

"I got the idea from Shadow. He kept avoiding gender terms when talking about our stalker."

"I must not be a good psychologist. I never wavered from thinking it was my patient."

"It was, in a way," Shadow said. "If not for him and his obsessions, I doubt his wife would be hunting you now. Daly said something interesting. He said she kept her house immaculate all the time."

"If he's right," Anya said, "I'd bet the wife knew about his obsessions and refused to play. Her mind probably broke when she found out her best friend didn't mind his dangerous games. The wife murdered them both, or he accidentally killed her friend and fled."

"What a mess, but I hope we're coming to an end, and she can be arrested and questioned. But if the body isn't her husband's, then he may still be the one after us. You two might still be wrong," Anais said.

"We'll have backup for tonight. At least, two outside and two in the restaurant. We'll call this off if either of you want me to. I'm going to let Commander Walsh know what's up. He may want to sit this one out."

"We're ready," Anya said. "I'll go with you. I want my life back."

"You all aren't leaving me behind. I'm not backing down either," Anais said.

Anya grinned. "She's getting more like me every day."

The commander and Shadow's mother said they were going with the rest of them.

"I haven't seen any real action in a while," the commander said. "I'm getting ready to retire. It'll be good to be in the middle of some action again. I'll have my gun in case it's needed."

"I don't like my mother being in danger."

"I'll put her on. I won't get in the middle between you two."

"Don't even say it," his mom told him. "I want to go to dinner. I'll have wonderful SEALs protecting me every moment."

"Mom, you'll be another person I have to worry about."

"We'll see you at six."

Shadow looked at his phone. He couldn't believe Mom had cut him off. "Damn." *That's it, I'm never getting married. I always thought Mom was the most reasonable woman I knew. But this shows me they can all be impossible.*

CHAPTER 10

Where could they have gone, and who is the man helping them? Damn, I need to get this finished and fly overseas. Wait! The man wore a uniform on one visit to their house. I'm going to stake out the area around the base. If I can find him, I'll find them.

Anais's neck muscles tightened. She tried to pretend to be at ease, but every time a waiter walked by or someone opened or shut a door, her anxiety increased. She glanced around the dining room full of people. Two men with short haircuts and a strong military bearing despite their casual clothes, sat at a table by the wall. She suspected they were their guards. Shadow's mom tried to keep the conversation going at their table, but no one was in the mood for talking.

Their waiter buzzed around them, bringing hors d'oeuvres and drinks. Mostly, they sipped the wine and nibbled at a few of the savory foods. Anais thought the evening would never end, but as time went by,

they began to relax, talk and enjoy their steaks.

"I want to tell you what a wonderful trip this has been so far," Rose said.

When they all finished, the commander insisted on paying for their meals. Then they walked outside. The parking lot was full. Shadow led the way, and the commander brought up the back.

Anais leaned toward her sister. "I feel like eyes are watching me."

"Don't be silly. It's your imagination. No idiot would attack us with Shadow, the commander, and two more SEALs bringing up the rear."

Once they were safely in the SUV, they headed toward Shadow's home. They turned onto the highway, and the commander sped up. He frowned and started to slow.

"What's the matter?" Shadow asked.

"The SUV's not driving right. I'm going to move

toward the edge of the road." When he turned the steering wheel, the SUV leaned toward one side. The sound of clunking and tearing filled the cab of the vehicle and it lurched abuptly. The women yelled. Anais saw a wheel roll across the lane beside them. Commander Walsh struggled to control the SUV.

Sparks spurted past Anais' window, she assumed from where the wheel assembly dragged on the road. Thankfully, the traffic slowed. Then shots came through the closed window. Shadow and the commander yelled, "Duck!" Shadow threw his body across the two twins huddling on the floor as shards of glass flew everywhere.

One of the two SEAL cars following Commander Walsh's SUV stopped briefly to let out one SEAL while the other one sped on ahead to try and catch up with the person who'd shot into the commander's car. The other SEAL ran toward the still moving SUV. Sirens sounded in the distance.

Once they stopped, Shadow sat up and checked everyone. The commander slumped over in his seat. A bullet had gone through his shoulder, and it bled quite profusely. Shadow's mother cried out and reached for him.

"How can I help?" the SEAl, who'd ran toward

their car, asked. Seeing the commander slumped over, he ran to his side and opened the door.

"Are either of you hurt?" Shadow asked the twins. "I see blood." He moved and looked down at Anais. "You're leg is bleeding."

"Not badly. The bullet must have hit the frame of the window and bounced off, hitting the upper part of my leg. It looks worse than it is."

"Damn, if it is the wife, she's a good shot to be able to drive at high speed and shoot at the same time."

"More lucky than talented," the commander said. "I'm glad to see we have three SEALs here to protect us until others get here." He nodded at the SEAL at his door and the other two who'd run up with guns drawn.

Shadow had taken off his shirt and handed it to the SEAL at the commander's side. "Put it against the commander's wound to slow the bleeding."

An ambulance stopped in front of them and the police pulled in behind the SUV. Shadow got out to explain.

"Do you know who shot at you?" the police officer asked.

"No, we suspect, but we didn't have time to see the driver or get a license plate number." Shadow gave them all the information he knew while the paramedics took care of the wounded.

When Shadow started toward the rescue vehicle, one of the paramedics stopped him. "We can take Commander Walsh to the Navy Hospital, but Ms. Kenly said she has to go to a civilian emergency room. We checked her vitals. She's stable. Luckily the bullet went right through from one side to the other. We've got another ambulance on the way, but we'd like to get the commander to the hospital."

"Go ahead. We'll be safe right here." Shadow nodded to the two SEALs from the other car. "They can handle anything."

The paramedic smiled. "I'd trust them with my life." She winked at the two men. They nodded but didn't smile.

One of the men stepped up. "Do you mind if I ride with the commander?"

"Not at all. I'm sure the commander will feel safer with a SEAL by his side."

"I'm going to be by his side." Shadow's mother moved forward. She looked at the paramedic and the SEAL. "But you two can find a place in the ambulance with us."

After they left, Shadow checked Anais's leg.

"You're lucky. It's a clean shot. They'll probably bandage your leg and put you on antibiotics."

"How do you know so much?" Anais asked. She smiled knowing he was right.

"We have to take care of each other out in the jungles, or wherever we go. We know some basic treatments."

"Handy," Anya said and smiled. "Is there anything you all can't do?"

"Lots, but we'd never admit it," he teased her. "Here comes our last ambulance." He picked Anais up and carried her to where the ambulance parked. He gently placed her on the stretcher. "We'll follow right behind."

He and Anya had barely gotten into the car with the SEAl's when Shadow's cell rang. "Hello."

"This is Chief Edwards. I just finished talking to Chief Daly in North Carolina. My medical examiner sent the sample off and asked for priority. I'll let you know the answer as soon as we hear."

"Thanks, we're going to need it."

Shadow thanked the Seals, and then he and Anya rushed into the emergency room. The staff had taken care of Anais's leg, bandaged it and were ready to send her off with antibiotics, as Shadow had predicted.

"I can walk with my crutches," Anais said when Shadow bent to pick her up.

"But I enjoy carrying you. Anya check and see if there's a taxi outside. If so, wave to me and go reserve it for us."

Once in the taxi it didn't seem to take long to get back to Shadow's home. "Stay still while I pay the taxi driver," he told Anais. "I've got it," Anya said and paid the driver.

Shadow carried Anais inside. "Your sister will bring the crutches. I'm taking you to my room. I want to check on you during the night and make certain you don't spike a fever."

"You know we can't fool around with my leg all bandaged."

"That's all right, but I think I can prove you wrong." He grinned. "But don't worry. I'd never hurt your leg or you in any way." He bent his head and kissed her.

She sighed. "Too bad this can't last."

"What do you mean?"

"Soon, you'll get the bad guy or woman and we'll be safe. I think Anya wants to move back to North Carolina and stay with Mom for a while." Anais cocked her head to the side. "Maybe not if she ends up liking her doctor, and wants to return. I suspect she may have reached out and made contact with him after her last visit. But at first we'll both spend time with Mom."

Shadow sat Anais on his bed. "Do you want to live in North Carolina again?"

"I can get a spot with the same group of doctors I worked with before all this happened. If I stayed in California, I'd have to jump through all the hoops to get my license."

"You can paint."

"My first love is being a doctor."

"Maybe I might convince you of the benefits of staying in California."

"We'll see. I'd want marriage and babies. I have a feeling you might not be ready for all of those responsibilities."

"Time will tell." He helped her get situated in bed and went out, shutting the door quietly behind him. Anya had closed her door. Shadow was glad. He let Scout out and when he returned, Shadow checked all the locks and then walked down the hall to his bedroom. He opened his door carefully and slipped inside. Anais had gone to sleep.

He put on his swim trunks, and took a pair of shorts and shirt for later. Once in the pool, he swam up and down the length, trying to quiet the unrest deep inside of him. Scout sat beside the pool watching him.

NICK, THE SEAL WHO HAD DRIVEN THE FIRST CAR behind the commander's SUV, continued down the road behind the vehicle involved in the attack on the SUV. Other drivers quickly got out of their way. The traffic thinned as they got further from San Diego and the towns around it. Nick slowed, hoping the other driver would quit going so fast and driving crazy. The sky darkened. A sudden downpour wet the roads. He slowed even more. The car ahead of him kept racing away.

The damn idiot won't slow down. I'll turn around. I got most of the tag number.

Nick drove back toward San Diego. He'd check on the commander and others, but he'd need to stop for gas before going any further. There were two stations at the next off-ramp. He turned left, stopped and filled the gas tank, then went inside for coffee.

The employee had a police scanner. There was static, but the garbled voices on it sounded shocked and were talking fast.

"What direction did you come from," the skinny young man asked.

"I'm headed for San Diego."

"Did you see the wreck?"

"No."

"Someone turned their car deliberately in front of a semi. I heard it on my scanner."

"I imagine it'd be a horrible sight to see." Nick paid him and walked outside. He debated about going back and decided to continue on to San Diego. If it was the same car he'd been trying to catch, there wasn't anything he could do now. He'd know soon enough. The eleven o'clock news would be full of talk about the crash.

But I'll call in and let my commander know what happened before he sees it on the news.

Why hadn't the person slowed? I pulled back before the crash.

After talking briefly to his commander, he called the Balboa Military Hospital and asked for the emergency room.

A nurse answered.

"I want to inquire about Commander Walsh's condition."

"Sorry," she said, politely but firmly. "We do not give information out over the phone." She hung up.

175

Damn, I knew better. Nick phoned Shadow.

"Hi, this is Nick from Paul's team. I wondered if the commander got admitted."

"Yes, they sent him to surgery right away. He may be out now. Can I help?"

"No. Thanks anyway."

SHADOW STARED AT HIS PHONE. WHY DID NICK END the call so fast? He checked at the hospital and rang the room where the commander was to go after surgery. His Mom answered.

"Is the commander all right?"

"Yes, not much damage was done. Larry's doctor said it might interfere with his golf swing. Larry's so out of it that it didn't faze him. He won't remember in the morning."

"I'm glad he'll be all right. Mom, are you certain about your feelings for the commander?"

"Yes. We make a good pair. Don't worry, we'll take our time. You and Anais can marry first."

"I'm not there yet, Mom."

"She's lovely and smart, and I think she loves you. What's the problem?"

"I'm a loner. I don't know how I'd do with

someone around all the time."

"You're worried you may die and leave a wife and your children alone. My grief affected you. Grief is a part of living. Few of us can avoid it. But it's what your father and I had before his death that counts."

"Maybe."

"I'd rather have had your Dad those years and gone through the grief than missed the joy we had together. I suspect your lady would say the same."

"Tell the commander I called and asked about him."

Shadow tiptoed down the hall so as not to disturb Anya. Spotting Scout, he motioned for him to go back to his bed in the family room. Shadow watched until Scout headed back that way. Scout stopped every few steps to be certain Shadow wouldn't change his mind and invite him into his room.

Shadow had to smile. It felt good to have his dog back home. He carefully opened his bedroom door and took off his clothes. Lifting the covers, he slid in beside Anais's warm body.

She turned and curled against him. He put his arms around her. In her sleep, she mumbled. "I love you." Her slow breathing ruffled the hair on his chest.

Those pain pills must have really knocked her out. What the hell am I going to do about her?

Toward morning, he woke in a cold sweat. He'd dreamed he raced through the jungle trying to find Anais. Laughter echoed around him. "You let her go. You let her go," the voices repeated.

He shuddered.

She woke and looked at him, bleary eyed. "Are you all right? You're shaking."

"I'm fine. I'll shower and fix breakfast."

"Won't you lay back down and hold me a few minutes?"

"I'm all sweaty. Maybe later." He rushed into the bathroom and let cold water run over his head and body. *What can I do? What do I want?*

When he came into the kitchen, Anais was finishing making a large omelet. Anya buttered toast. Shadow poured himself a cup of coffee and sat at the small table on one side of the kitchen.

"It smells good in here."

Anais handed him a glass of orange juice and then filled their plates with a third of the omelet and bacon, and put toast on a small side plate. "Eat up."

"I'm hungrier than I thought," Shadow said and dug in.

CHAPTER 11

Chief Edwards looked at the date their forensic laboratory had sent. They estimated it would be two months or more before they received the results, and the supervisor had added a note that if the man had been dead for some time, and no one in the area was missing, they didn't see a need to move his DNA up in line.

He slammed the paper down on his desk and swore. His secretary, who'd brought in the letter, jumped.

"Sorry, Mabel. But the slowness of our lab is irritating. Did we keep any DNA locked up?"

"Yes. Since you worry so often about it getting lost, Darryl decided to keep some extra DNA safe and locked up on each case."

"Darryl's an excellent officer. Tell him I may want the DNA on this case sent to an independent lab. Tell him not go home until I make this call."

"Yes, Sir."

Chief Daly was closing his office door when he heard his phone. He started to let it ring, then grimaced. It might be important. Grumbling, he went back in, snatched up the reciever.

"Hello, Chief Daly."

"I'm glad I caught you, chief. This is Chief Edwards from Pensacola."

"I guess it's too soon to have found your body's identity."

"Yes, and our labs are understaffed. They estimate over two months for results. I wondered if you might get it done faster."

"I'll call a friend in Raleigh. He sometimes manages to get DNA checked quickly, if it's important."

"Great. It's nice to know people in the right jobs. Call me if it's sooner than two months. I can have a man deliver samples in person wherever they need to go."

"I'm trying to solve a murder and a disappearance. It'd help to find out the results sooner than two months. Let me give you my private number, but give me an hour or two before you call."

"Will do."

SHADOW HAD FINISHED EATING WHEN HIS CELL RANG. "Hello, Captain. I hope you're calling to say the commander is doing well."

"He's going to be fine, but that's not why I called. Nick got in touch with me late last night. I'm not sure you were aware one of the SEALs following the commander's SUV went after the shooter."

"No, so much was happening, I didn't even notice."

"Nick followed the car out of San Diego but backed off when the driver kept getting more reckless. He turned around and stopped to get gas. The man at the register told Nick he'd heard on a police scanner about an accident involving a reckless driver and a semi.

"What happened to the car?"

"Drivers who saw it all said the car deliberately swung in front of a semi-truck. The semi driver was shook up, but he'll be all right. The woman in the car died. I think the twins are safe now."

Shadow sat down. "Why would she deliberately kill herself?"

"Maybe she knew we'd get her soon and didn't want to face the media and a trial, and going to jail for possibly life. It's weird, but she did have her ID in her purse. They're still going to check the DNA, so there'll be no doubt concerning her identity."

"And the ID was of the councilman's wife, Marian Steen?"

"Yes, it had her address in North Carolina."

"Anais and Anya are right beside me. I'll give them the news. Thanks."

The captain asked, "Do you want to take the next week as vacation or join the team?"

"I'll fly out tomorrow."

Shadow turned to Anais and her sister. "I'm sure you heard enough to understand the woman after you killed herself in an accident with a semi."

Anais sat down. "Why would she do something so horrible to herself?"

"She knew capture, trial, and jail were in front of her. I expect it was an instant thought and she reacted too quickly to change her mind."

Anya went white. "All because her stupid husband left her and wanted a divorce. She probably thought everyone in town knew of his weird obsessions. I'd bet if they ever had any love between them, it disappeared long ago. All she had was her standing in town as the councilman's wife. I almost pity her, except for how she messed with Anais and me and tried her best to kill us."

"It's over, and I have to join my team tomorrow. You can stay here at my place, or I'll help you move back home. I'm going to have Scout stay with my mother and the commander until I'm back and settled."

Anais stood. "We'll move our few things home to North Carolina. Then we'll fly there to see Mom. She'll want to see us safe and sound. We can take our time deciding our future." With tears in her eyes, Anais walked past Shadow to the room she'd only used to change clothes.

Anya looked from her sister to Shadow. "What did you do to her?"

"Nothing. I realized I'm not ready to marry. I have to pull away before I hurt Anais more."

"Ah. You aren't as smart as I thought." Anya walked briskly down the hall.

I hope I didn't just make the biggest mistake of my life.

❋

Shadow helped with their suitcases. An awkward silence surrounded them in the car on the way to their house. "I hope you have a great visit with your Mom. I'll call when I get back from my mission."

Anais picked up her suitcase and headed toward her bedroom. Over her shoulder, she said, "Don't bother."

"I'm sorry I upset her," Shadow said to Anya. "But I can't rush into anything."

"Don't say any more. She needs time to heal from you and this woman who almost killed us. I appreciate all you did, but you need to stay away and let her find the life she had before.

"Anais is beautiful, kind, and deserves someone to love her completely. If you don't want a life with her, you did the best thing by ending it now. Thank you for saving our lives and freeing us from this awful experience. For that, Anais and I will be forever grateful." She smiled slightly. "Now go save some of the rest of the world." Anya hugged him and opened the front door, wordlessly asking him to leave.

Unable to think of anything to say, Shadow leaned down and kissed her cheek. He hurried out to his car and sped away.

Anais, standing in front of her bedroom window shielded by curtains, cried as she watched his car go out of sight. Anya walked into her room and hugged her.

"Half-asleep, I told him I loved him." She tried to smile, but it came out a grimace. "I guess it scared him and he pulled away."

"It's good he's leaving. I think when he returns, he'll contact you. It's up to you whether you want to answer his call."

Two Months Later

The plane landed at one A.M. Ranger laughed when he looked at his teammates. "What a motley crew," he said. "I'm going home to sleep, and then get a haircut. Are we meeting at Ace's tonight?"

"Sure thing," Gordy said. "The wives like getting together, and we do, too. How about you, Bear?"

"We'll see. Kayla and I will decide whether tomorrow night or the night after. Get some rest. We did our job and earned our downtime." The back door opened and the guys went down the ramp and hurried across the tarmac to either their wife, girl-friend or car.

Shadow waved and headed to his truck. *I wonder if Mom's still at the commander's house. I know she planned to stay at least until he completely recovered from the gunshot wound. I'll call in the morning and arrange to pick up Scout.*

At home, he parked the truck in his garage, unlocked the door to the kitchen and walked inside. The house had an empty feeling. He'd never before thought of it as cold and empty. He grabbed a beer out of the fridge and went into the family room. After lighting a fire, he sat on the sofa.

He tried to keep Anais out of his thoughts while on the mission. But whenever he was back in camp, alone at night, it was impossible.

Shadow closed his eyes and wished for sleep. Maybe a hot shower would help. He ignored his bed and went into the bathroom. He let the warm water run over him for a long time, then got out, dried off, and headed to bed.

I changed the sheets before I left, but I swear I can smell her scent. Shadow tossed and turned for an hour before getting up and putting on shorts.

Outside, the moon shone bright, and a cool breeze blew over his body. He grabbed another cold beer on the way out. He took a sip and lay on the cushioned lounger by the pool. Shadow practiced the meditation his mother taught him and gradully his body relaxed, and he slept.

Anya glanced across the kitchen table at her sister. "I got an email from Caroline. She said Shadow's team got back a few nights ago."

"Why do you keep in touch with her? We've both decided to stay in North Carolina. I can't believe you want to be an author, but I bet you'll do good. I'm even looking forward to accepting the position with the Terrell-Baskin Internist group in Raleigh. It looks promising."

"I keep in touch with Caroline to know what's happening with the teams. Also, I've been in communication with a certain Dr. Lars Andrews. I'm going to fly to San Diego and have that date we missed."

"I thought you'd forgotten about him."

"No, I contacted him and we've stayed in touch. Why don't you fly to San Diego with me next Thursday? Lars said he has plenty of room for both of us at his house." Anya laughed. "You can be my chaperone."

Anais turned and walked to the front room window. "I don't know if I'm ready to leave Mom."

Their mother cleared her throat. "I missed most of the conversation, but I insist you make your own decisions on what you want without considering me. I'm fine here. I can visit wherever you two go, but this is my home. I'm comfortable here."

"Think about it, Anais," Anya said. "I'm going downtown to buy a new computer. I'm tired of writing longhand."

"I'll go with you," Anais said.

Anais enjoyed watching her sister go through the local computer store. She checked every computer before deciding on the second one she'd scrutinized.

As they came out of the store, they saw Chief Daly headed in their direction.

"I heard the two of you were in town. Can we go to my office and talk?" he asked.

"Join us at the tea shop across the street," Anya said.

The chief glanced at his watch. "I'd rather talk with you later in my office. I wanted to catch you and your sister before you head out to your mother's ranch."

"We don't mind you having tea with us. We're interested in what you have to say," Anais said.

It's very private information. Come to my office after you have your tea."

"Now you have our curiosity up. We'll come with you and get our tea later."

Once they were settled in the Chief's office and he'd told his secretary to hold all calls, the Chief began to talk.

"I'm going to tell you more information than I should, but I feel after what you two went through you have a right to know why she wanted to kill you. You must not tell anyone else this information."

"We won't. We promise," Anya said and Anais nodded her head.

"Good, I'm going to hold you to that promise. It took us some time to get the DNA results. The body in Pensacola was the councilman. I had the scarf from around the neck of our strangled victim checked. The DNA found on it was the victim's and the councilman's wife."

"Wow, she was on a murdering rampage," Anais said.

"Yes. From what I've gathered from talking to Marian's close friends, she found out about the affair between her husband and her best friend. Then he comes home one day and tells her he wants a divorce and he's moving to Florida.

"My men checked around the house and found some evidence of blood in the bedroom. I figure she killed him, somehow transported the body to the woods near Pensacola, drove back and killed her friend."

"I bet she thought no one would consider her as the villain," Anya said.

"No one except possibly you, Anya, and she maybe thought you'd told your sister about your patient. You knew about Marian's husband's obsessions. Her biggest fear must have been that someone in town would find out about him and tell others.

"We think Marian killed her best friend for her betrayal and as revenge on her husband for leaving town. Maybe she suspected the friend planned to join him at a later date. No one knows what thoughts were in her head."

"And that's why she came after me?" Anya asked. "And Anais."

"I talked to her cousin in Arizona. She did visit her, and the cousin was glad to see Marian leave.

"After she left, the cousin found a notebook. The cousin sent me the book after I contacted her. In it, she feared you two were the only ones, other than herself and her dead friend, who knew about her husband's obsessions and sexual fantasies.

"She wanted to come back home, live her life out, and not worry you'd return one day and tell someone about him."

The sheriff sat back. "Her husband's family had money and position in this town. I don't know for certain, but I think she loved the prestige of being the wife of a councilman. She didn't want to lose the only thing that mattered."

"It doesn't seem that a councilman's wife is that important," Anais said.

"She was a rigid, unhappy lady. Any change was difficult for her. I was in school with them and noticed her hangups even then." He shook his head. "I'm sorry my detective didn't believe you about him being dangerous. He wasn't, in many ways, but when he started the ball rolling, it ran right over him." Chief Daly lowered his head. "It's all a sad mess."

Anya put her hand on his. "You aren't to blame for what they did. I wish your detective had believed me."

"I've learned a difficult lesson. I've instructed my new detective that if you or someone else comes to him like you did that time, he'd better report it to me right away. No matter how important the person may seem or even if he's a friend. He's just moved here, so hopefully he'll do as I said. Are you two staying here at your Mom's house?"

"Not for long. I'm moving away and plan to write scary mystery books. I'll send my first published book to you," Anya said.

"I'm not certain of my future," Anais told him. "I have time to make some decisions."

He shook their hands. "Anya, I'll be looking for that book."

They left and went back to the tea shop. "What a crazy story. If I wrote about this, no one would believe me." Anya took a sip of her tea, and a bite of her scone.

"From what you told the Chief, I gather you like the doctor, and you plan on living in San Diego."

"Yes, I guess I do. When I reached out to him, he was receptive to keeping in touch. We've been writing and he's called a few times. It will feel strange for you and I to be apart for the first time in our lives."

"Maybe we can find what we want easier living seperately than living together. I'll come to visit, but first I'll let you get settled."

"You may be there sooner than you think.

Shadow had feelings for you. They scared him, but he'll get over it and call."

"I don't think he will. I told him I loved him. He turned and ran away fast. I'm taking some more time off before I decide where I want to be in practice. I'll stay with Mom. She likes my paintings. We'll share her studio and see what happens."

"I hate seeing you sad."

"Not sad so much as resigned." Anais smiled and patted her sister's hand. "As the older sister by five minutes, you can't always make things right for me."

"I knew you'd remind me I'm older than you." Anya hugged Anais. "I love you, Sis."

"I love you, too."

CHAPTER 12

Shadow roamed around his empty house. He'd been back for two days, but the peace he'd enjoyed on his return from previous missons eluded him.

I made a terrible mistake. When Anais said she loved me, I ran away both mentally and physically.

His cell rang, and he grabbed for it. Anything to keep his thoughts away. "Hi, Mom. How are you?"

"Very well. After you left for your mission, Larry and I decided to visit my home in Montana. I wanted him to meet our family. Everyone likes him. Later, we headed to his brother's house, which as you know isn't far from mine."

"Are you having a good time?"

"So much that we've decided we'll get married.

Larry has put in for retirement. We'll travel and enjoy the rest of our lives together."

"Marry? Isn't this quick?"

"I married your Dad after knowing him for three months. Something inside tells me when I've found the right man. I'll give Larry the phone. He wants to speak with you."

"Hello, Shadow. I wanted to reassure you I will love and take good care of your mother the rest of my life. We both feel very lucky to have found someone to love again. Not everyone gets that chance.

"What your mother and I feel for each other doesn't take anything away from the love and relationship we had with our previous spouse. I feel incrediably lucky that Rose has agreed to marry me."

"I hope you both will be very happy, commander."

"Please, call me Larry. If that's too informal, try Lawrence."

"It'll take some time to get used to, Sir."

"I understand. I've met your sister and your uncles. They've given us their blessing, as has my brother. I hope you will, too."

"I want my mother to be happy. All of this will

take some time for me to adjust to, but I have no doubt you'll be good to her."

"Thank you. Your mother wants to speak with you again."

"We want to be married while you're home. What do you think about two weeks from today?"

"Quick."

His mom laughed. Shadow realized how long it had been since she had laughed out loud. Mostly, it had been a chuckle or a smile.

"I'll be there. Where are you getting married?"

"We thought San Diego. Larry has many friends there. Our families are willing to make a trip to see the wedding and the city. In fact, they're looking forward to it."

"I have extra bedrooms. The single uncles can stay with me."

"Great. Talk to you soon."

Shadow shook his head and then grinned. *I won't be lonely much longer. But I have something I want to do right now.*

ANAIS'S MOTHER SAT DOWN BESIDE HER DAUGHTER

while Anais finished her breakfast. "What are your plans for today?"

"Nothing much. I'm going riding down to the creek. Maybe I'll catch a fish."

"And throw it back, as usual." Her mother smiled.

"Yes, it's the fun of the catch. I don't want to kill it and eat it."

Her mother pulled Anais's chair and hers around until they sat face to face. She held Anais's hand.

"I worry about you. You've been home almost four months and haven't looked for a job. Your old group has contacted you, and they said to come to work whenever you are ready."

"I know."

"Is it about the man you left in California?"

"Perhaps, a little."

"Then take the boards for California and go back. You can live with your sister and her fiance. I must admit the quick engagement surprised me. It's not at all like Anya."

"When I saw them together, it was obvious they were made for each other. Anya's doctor knows how to handle her. I didn't know if she'd find the right one. Of course, Anya would say Lars doesn't handle her."

"I was positive you would be the first to marry."

"Mom, you can't be right all the time." Anais hugged her mother. "I'm glad we've had time to spend together. I'll start thinking about my future. I'm going out to saddle Cherry. See you later."

"I'll be in my studio, painting."

Cherry nudged Anais as she saddled the horse. "I know you like getting to ride more since I've been home. If I stay in this area, I'll be able to take you out often."

She swung her leg over the saddle and headed for the creek. Cherry knew the way, so Anais took her time enjoying the sight of the spring flowers and the open land surrounding her.

After she'd caught three fish and thrown them back, she leaned against a large tree and closed her eyes. The gentle breeze and quiet lulled her to sleep.

SHADOW TIED HIS HORSE A GOOD WAYS FROM WHERE he saw the sparkle of water. Ms. Kenly had told him how to find Anais and gave him the impression her daughter would be happy to see him. *I hope she's right.*

He quietly slipped between the trees and found

her sound asleep. It was a lovely, peaceful area. Shadow got off his horse and leaned forward to brush a light kiss across her lips.

Anais stirred and opened her eyes. "I must be in bad shape to imagine I'm seeing Kijika riding one of our horses."

"No, my darling. I'm here. Your mother let me use one the horses." He leaned down and kissed the top of her head. "I missed you, a lot."

"You can't be the Shadow I knew. He's determined to run away from love or any commitment."

Shadow knelt at her feet. "I love you, Anais. You haunted me while I was on my mission. I can't enjoy my house anymore without you in it. When you surprised me and said you loved me, I ran as fast and as far as I could. But you followed me. I couldn't outrun my heart and how I felt about you."

She started to grin. "Can I put my recorder on when we get back and have you say all of that again? I'd like to play it for my mother, my sister, your mother and sister, and anyone else who might like to tease you."

He grinned, pulled her up and spun her around. "Never. Will you marry me?"

"I guess I have to. I'm miserable without you."

"My sweet Anais, I don't plan to leave you again

except on missions. Then we'll have a wonderful homecoming every time I return."

They sat back down under the tree with Shadow behind her and his arms wrapped around her. He kissed her neck. "I like your state. It's beautiful."

"It is, but wherever you are is all right with me. With no one chasing Anya and me, we can visit Mom anytime."

"Maybe she'd like to come live with us. It'd be company for you while I'm gone."

"No, Mom will never leave this ranch. She loves it, and her horses and her paintings. She'll visit. How about your mother?"

"Mom is marrying Commander Walsh in about a week and a half."

"Is that why you came to propose to me? You wanted to one-up your mother?"

"No, silly. But it did make me realize that I could lose you forever. I want to marry the woman I love with all my heart and not worry about our future. And by the way I liked it when you called me Kijika. I'd like for you to call me by my name more often."

"I started to several times, but you were our Seal protector and some how it didn't seem right until now.

Anais held his hands and asked, "Why were you so determined not to marry?"

"When Dad died, Mom was a wreck. They'd planned so many fun things to do after he retired, and that wasn't going to happen. She lost him and all their dreams for the future. Just before his retirement, he got killed. She'd always been a strong person, but she went to pieces."

"How awful."

"Yes, and as her only son, I couldn't leave her. I'd planned to enlist in the Navy right after graduation and try out for the SEALs as soon as possible."

"But you didn't?"

"No, I taught in the school on the reservation for two years. Finally, my mother and my grandfather convinced me to follow my dreams."

"How did your mother do?"

"All right. Over the years she became more like her old self. But it wasn't until I heard the joy in her voice when she talked about the commander and the laughter that I knew she'd fully embraced life again. She and the commander are getting married next Saturday. I want you by my side."

Anais glanced down at the lovely diamond ring as he slid it on her finger.

Shadow's forehead wrinkled. "You look worried?"

"Why did you ask me to marry you now?"

"For the reasons I said. I thought about you all the time at our base camp. Not when I was out working, but I knew right after you'd left I'd made a big mistake.

"I feared if I married and got killed, you'd suffer like my mother. I didn't want that for you."

"It would be my choice." She shrugged her shoulders. "You didn't talk it over with me."

"I just ran."

Anais bit her lip to keep from laughing at the anxious expression on his face, but he had to suffer for a few minutes. "Yes, you did, far, far away. No messages, no nothing."

"We couldn't call or write from where we were located. Our missions are secret. When we leave, even as a wife you won't know where I am or when I'm coming home. If we have children, you'll be mom and dad until I return. The divorce rate is high among SEALs. Can you handle that? Eventually, I'll retire, but not yet."

"Are you trying to scare me off?"

He hugged her. "No way. But I don't want you to go into this with me unless you understand it all."

As he stood, Shadow pulled her up with him. She grabbed his collar and brought his face closer to hers. "Look, buddy. You've proposed. I've got your ring on my finger, and I am not letting you off the hook"—she glanced at the river—"like I do my fish."

He picked her up in his arms and kissed her. "Shall we make love first or go right away and tell your mom about our plans?"

Anais glanced around the open area except for the trees. "Dare we?"

"Yes." Before she could change her mind, he pulled Anais's shirt over her head and flung it and her bra to the side. The cool breeze made her nipples tighten. Shadow cupped her breasts in his hands and leaned down to kiss each one.

A tiny glow spread from under her breast throughout her body. She tingled with joy.

His sharp eyes studied her face, the skin on his lean, cheeks as rich as caramel and just as tantalizing. "I love you." He spoke clearly and stared into her eyes, before he bent and kissed her forehead, her cheeks, and captured her mouth with a deep hunger. His tongue tasted every spot, and he gently bit the edge of her lip when as he started to move down.

"You're trembling. Wait." Shadow hurried to his

horse and unwrapped the blanket he'd brought with him. He spread the comforter over a grassy spot.

"Where did you get my comforter?"

"Your Mom rushed off and came back with it. I blushed, and she laughed, saying I might need it."

Anais's face flushed hot red. "My mother? Wait until I see her."

"I hope you'll say thanks. I will." Shadow put out his hand. "Join me?"

"How can I resist?" Anais unbuttoned his shirt and spread her hands across his tanned chest. She leaned in and took a deep breath of his scent. Then she raised her head and said, "You'd better not ever leave me."

His face reflected the seriousness of his answer. "I promise never to leave you unless there is no way to get back, and I will not give up trying to return to you until I take my last breath."

Tears ran down Anais's face. Shadow kissed them away. "I'll try my best to see we grow old together."

She kissed his nipples, his wide chest, and up his neck to his mouth. "Let's get naked and love each other."

"I thought you'd never get around to our sexy exploration."

"You are so bad, only thinking of one thing," she teased and pulled him into her arms.

He tasted and kissed his way down her body. The mere touch of Shadow's hand sent a warming shiver throughout her body. He kissed her most sensitive spot. Then he raised his head and looked into her eyes. "Are you ready for me, my love?" he asked.

Her heart pounded in her chest, and excitement raced through her veins. She couldn't speak, only nod.

SHADOW REACHED FOR HIS NEARBY PANTS AND PULLED out a condom. Once in place, he stared into her eyes as he entered her warmth. He moved slowly at first, savoring the emotions flooding his body. Watching the emotions cross her face, his movements quickened until they both reached a pinnacle of joy and for a second all the world went away, and only Anais and him existed.

Shadow rolled over, bringing her with him to cuddle against his side. "I liked that. We must do it more often." He leaned over and smiled at her sweet face. "Don't you agree?"

"Most definitely." She brushed his hair off his forehead.

"Happy?"

"Of course. Can't you tell from my expression?"

"Just wanted to verify I was right."

He lay on his side and picked up her hand, running his finger over the stone on her ring finger. "I bought this at a strange shop. Bear and Heath urged me to go there. The proprietor sold me the set. He said to tell you it would bring much love and many children to us, and protect us in times of danger."

"It's beautiful. I love the large emerald. The diamonds around it makes it glow."

"According to the jeweler, it turns almost black to warn you of danger. The wedding ring is a mixture of diamonds and emeralds, but the stones aren't as large as in this engagement ring. It fits snug against your engagement ring." He leaned down and kissed her ring finger. "My ring is rather plain, but has three small diamonds on the top, one for you, one for me,and one for our children. He's quite a character. I told him we'd stop by if you accepted my proposal. He said not to worry.

"We'll go see him when we get back. I thought we'd spend tomorrow with your mom. I'll invite her to my mother's wedding to meet all the family. She can fly with us when we leave in two days or come just before my mother's and the commander's wedding."

"She'll choose the latter. Mom hates to be away from home for long."

"Doesn't she get lonely?"

"She has her paintings and her lover."

"What?" Shadow grinned.

"He's a professor at one of the universities in Raleigh. They met after his wife died, about a year after Dad's death. Mom took one of his courses for fun. She kept him at arm's length until we had to leave and were in danger. He became her support and lover. I tease her, but she said she's still not ready to marry. I think he'll wear her down."

"I'd like to meet him."

"Oh, that's not possible. Mom's mother was strict. If alive, she'd be shocked at her daughter's behavior. No one knows about Mom's friend except my sister and me. We met him briefly one time at the ranch."

"What would your Dad say?"

"Pretty lady, you are still alive. I'm gone. Enjoy your life and live it to the fullest."

"My life was much less complicated before all

you women, including my mother, came into my life and shook it up."

"Are you sorry?"

He pulled her to lay across his body. "Hell, no. Let's make love one more time before leaving this nice spot."

Anais chuckled as he rolled her under him. "A great idea."

CHAPTER 13

ANAIS STRAIGHTENED HER SISTER'S GOWN IN THE BACK. "You make a beautiful bride, Anya."

"Who thought I'd end up marrying a doctor."

"I did. The sparks flew whenever you two were around each other."

"And he loves that I'm writing murder mysteries. He always reads them before they go to the editor. He's good at catching my mistakes, and of course, he's my most loyal fan."

Anais handed her sister the white bouquet with white roses and a large white orchid in the center. "I'm going to peek outside and see if mom's arrived. I thought she'd be here by now. We wanted to bring her, but she said she'd come by cab. I think she may be picking up your present."

A number of their more recent friends from the hospital where Anya's fiance worked and some of Kijika's and Anais's friends were already seated. The organist played soft music as more family and guests arrived. Anais didn't see her mother anywhere. She frowned and started back up the aisle. As she got to the doors of the church, they opened.

Her mother and a handsome white-haired man entered. "Mom, I started to worry about you."

"I went to the airport to pick up my surprise. Anais, I'm sure you remember meeting Professor James once before, and this time I'd like you to meet him as as my new husband, Raymond James."

Anais's mouth dropped open.

"Dear, it isn't attractive to have your mouth wide open."

"I'm in shock, but"—she turned to address the man at her mother's side—"I'm so glad to meet you again. Mom, you did surprise me. Wait until I tell Anya."

"Don't. I'll tell Anya at the reception. Let her keep her mind on her wedding."

"It will be difficult, but I'll try. Oh, and here is Shadow's mom and her new husband." Anais did the introductions and watched as the two couples walked down the aisle and sat together.

"Is Mom here?" Anya asked when Anais joined her.

"Yes. She's sitting with Rose and Larry."

"Oh, good." Anya looked at her watch. "Thank goodness it's time." Anais opened the door and walked down the aisle in front of her sister.

At the reception, Kijika came up behind Anais and put his arms around her. "Your sister looked stunned when your mother introduced her husband."

"No more than I did when I met them coming into the church." Anais turned in his arms.

"We're the last to tie the knot. We are going to marry, aren't we?"

"Absolutely. But I don't want all this fancy stuff. Would you be hurt if we got married while both parents are here? We can go to the courthouse and my mom will insist on having a lovely after-wedding dinner at her home here in San Diego. She and Larry will be heading out soon to go to Mom's house to see all the brothers, and then drive onward to visit his brother and family."

He studied her face closely. "If you can't live without all of this, we'll do it up fancy."

Anais leaned forward and whispered, "I was dreading this. Your plan for our wedding sounds delightfully less stressful than the fancy wedding others expect we'll have. And the parents won't have to fly back so soon. I'm the third to marry, and I'm not waiting much longer for you to make an honest woman of me."

Shadow swung her around. "Have I told you how much I love you?"

Anais giggled. "Not in the last hour."

"Then let's leave here and make our plans. I've already asked mom to speak with your mother and her husband. All I have to do is wave to her, like this."

After wishing her sister and new brother-in-law much happiness, they slipped out and headed home. On the way, they stopped for pizza.

"Do you want Bourbon and Coke or wine with the pizza?" Kijika asked.

"Neither. I made tea. I'll have a glass of that."

"Don't get up. I'll get it. You look a little pale. Are you sure you're all right?"

"I may not be."

"What's the matter." he knelt by her chair. "Do you need to see the doctor?"

"No, I'll be fine in about seven and a half months."

Kijika looked puzzled.

"Everyone else may have beaten us to the altar, but we will be the first to have a baby."

Kijika didn't look any more enlightened. Anais watched his face closely. Slowly a grin crossed his face. His hand touched her belly. "We're having a baby?"

"Yes, the day I forgot my pills has shown how quickly I can get pregnant. You remember. I worried you'd be upset and you calmed me down. But neither of us thought one day might make such a difference."

"Wow, our baby." He picked her up and twirled her around. Seeing her expression, he put her back in the chair fast.

"Did I hurt you?"

"My stomach can't take twirling. I thought you'd be a little upset about my being pregnant so soon."

"Nope, that crazy jeweler was right. He said we'd have many children, and we'd start quickly."

"You believed him?"

"There are mysteries we can't understand. I believe this jeweler is a gifted man."

"I want to meet him. But I hope he doesn't tell me I'm having twins. We ran our poor mother to death until we started school. Anya and I were into everything."

"Maybe they'll take after me and be peaceful.

Laughing, she swatted at his shoulder and leaned forward to kiss him.

EPILOGUE

SURROUNDED BY BOTH SETS OF PARENTS IN THE hospital room, Kijika held his son in his arms. The grandparents beamed at their grandson, Brodie Kijika Gibson.

"Brodie was the name of a dear friend of mine. He didn't make it back from one of our missions about five years ago. I've contacted his parents and invited them to visit and meet our son named for their's."

His mother beamed at Anais's mother. "I'm honored our granddaughter has our names, Dacey Rose Gibson."

Anais grinned at all the grandparents. "I hope you'll visit when Kijika's gone on mission. I'll need lots of help. I remember what a difficult time we gave my mother."

Later, when all the company had gone, Anais handed her daughter to the nurse, who placed her in the crib near the bed. Brodie had gone asleep in his father's arms, but Dacey looked all around.

"She is going to give us a lot of joy and many headaches. I think she'll behave like my sister and I did until we went to school. We had a very stern teacher who taught us to behave or we'd have to stay late at school."

"We can handle Dacey." He nodded to Brodie. "I think he takes after me."

"I never should have suggested we might have twins. I think someone up above is laughing."

"Your sister gave me some good news to tell you after everyone left. They're expecting in about seven months."

Anais looked upward. "Did You hear that? Give her twins, too."

"Oh, you are mean," Kijika teased.

"I'm really happy we have twins. Just a bit afraid they'll stick together when you're on a mission and test my patience."

"Call your mother for help. She raised you two."

"We lived in the country during the years when we grew up. We'd have gotten into a lot more mischief if we didn't have the ranch and horses, and fishing."

Kijika leaned down and kissed her. "Sleep. You did a lot of work bringing our pair into the world. I'll sleep in that nice soft recliner over by the window."

When he started to move away, Anais pulled on his arm. He leaned back down. "I love you, Kijika, and I also love Shadow."

"My heart is full with you and our babies. I'm going to be ribbed by the guys. I swore I'd never get married. They are going to laugh up a storm to hear we are a family of four."

"Do you care?"

"No, I think it'll be great fun."

She caught his hand. "When do you have to leave on another mission?"

"Not today. But it could be any day. Mom said she'd stay with you until you were on your feet and stronger."

"Let's hope we have a few weeks, my dear husband."

"I agree. I know all the grandparents will gather around and see that you and the babies are taken care of until I return. I expect Scout will run between you and the twins to make sure everything is all right. He's been constantly beside you since we got him back. He may be older, but he'll protect his family."

Dacey Rose cried out and waved her hands and feet. Her cry woke Brodie, but he just looked around. Kijika lifted his daughter into his arms. Anais knew the newborn couldn't see more than shadows, but she seemed to stare up at his face as her small fingers wrapped around his finger.

"I knew it." Anais laughed. "I wish you could see your expression. When she put her fingers around yours, Daddy's heart got wrapped around her little finger."

"You're right, but Brodie's gone back to sleep. Do you think we'll have twins again next time?"

Joy filled his heart as his loving wife hit him with a pillow.

"Now look what you've done. You said it out loud."

Dacey stopped crying and watched her laughing father.

"Good night, my lovely lady. I'm in complete control here."

"Some control," Anais said with a smirk, as Dacey started to fuss again.

THE END

BOOKS BY RACHEL MCNEELY

Born in Florida, Rachel McNeely's early dreams included being a movie star. Of course, it didn't happen. Later, she escaped into daydreams full of fascinating stories. Her friends had to endure her reading those tales to them when she began to put them to paper.

There were detours in her life for marriage, children, and going back to college. But, she continued to be an avid reader and dream of the day she'd have a book published. Once her children were grown and she had time to write, she joined a writer's group and her dreams of writing and publishing came true.

f facebook.com/RachelMcNeelyAuthor

a amazon.com/Rachel-McNeely

BB bookbub.com/authors/rachel-mcneely

More Books in the Special Forces: Operation Alpha World!
See all the books at www.AcesPress.com

Melissa Combs: Gallant

KaLyn Cooper: Rescuing Melina

Liz Crowe: Marking Mariah

Jordan Dane: Redemption for Avery

Jordan Dane: Fiona's Salvation

Riley Edwards: Protecting Olivia

Riley Edwards: Redeeming Violet

Riley Edwards, Recovering Ivy

Nicole Flockton: Protecting Maria

Nicole Flockton: Guarding Erin

Nicole Flockton: Guarding Suzie

Nicole Flockton: Guarding Brielle

Casey Hagen: Shielding Nebraska

Casey Hagen: Shielding Harlow

Casey Hagen: Shielding Josie

Casey Hagen: Shielding Blair

Desiree Holt: Protecting Maddie

Kathy Ivan: Saving Sarah

Kathy Ivan: Saving Savannah

Kathy Ivan: Saving Stephanie

Jesse Jacobson: Protecting Honor

Jesse Jacobson: Fighting for Honor

Jesse Jacobson: Defending Honor

Jesse Jacobson: Summer Breeze

Silver James: Rescue Moon

Silver James: SEAL Moon

LeTeisha Newton: Protecting Butterfly
LeTeisha Newton: Protecting Goddess
LeTeisha Newton: Protecting Vixen
LeTeisha Newton: Protecting Heartbeat
MJ Nightingale: Protecting Beauty
MJ Nightingale: Betting on Benny
MJ Nightingale: Protecting Secrets
Sarah O'Rourke: Saving Liberty
Debra Parmley: Protecting Pippa
Lainey Reese: Protecting New York
Jenika Snow: Protecting Lily
Jen Talty: Burning Desire
Jen Talty: Burning Kiss
Jen Talty: Burning Skies
Jen Talty: Burning Lies
Jen Talty: Burning Heart
Megan Vernon: Protecting Us
Megan Vernon: Protecting Earth

Fire and Police: Operation Alpha World

Cara Carnes: Protecting Mari
KaLyn Cooper: Justice for Gwen

As you know, this book included at least one character from Susan Stoker's books. To check out more, see below.

Delta Force Heroes Series
Rescuing Rayne (FREE!)
Rescuing Aimee (novella)
Rescuing Emily
Rescuing Harley
Marrying Emily
Rescuing Kassie
Rescuing Bryn
Rescuing Casey
Rescuing Sadie
Rescuing Wendy
Rescuing Mary (Oct 2018)
Rescuing Macie (April 2019)

Badge of Honor: Texas Heroes Series
Justice for Mackenzie (FREE!)
Justice for Mickie
Justice for Corrie
Justice for Laine (novella)
Shelter for Elizabeth
Justice for Boone

Shelter for Adeline

Shelter for Sophie

Justice for Erin

Justice for Milena

Shelter for Blythe

Justice for Hope (Sept 2018)

Shelter for Quinn (Feb 2019)

Shelter for Koren (June 2019)

Shelter for Penelope (Oct 2019)

SEAL of Protection Series

Protecting Caroline (FREE!)

Protecting Alabama

Protecting Fiona

Marrying Caroline (novella)

Protecting Summer

Protecting Cheyenne

Protecting Jessyka

Protecting Julie (novella)

Protecting Melody

Protecting the Future

Protecting Kiera (novella)

Protecting Dakota

SEAL of Protection: Legacy Series

Securing Caite (Jan 2019)

Securing Sidney (May 2019)
Securing Piper (Sept 2019)
Securing Zoey (TBA)
Securing Avery (TBA)
Securing Kalee (TBA)

New York Times, *USA Today* and *Wall Street Journal* Bestselling Author Susan Stoker has a heart as big as the state of Texas where she lives, but this all American girl has also spent the last fourteen years living in Missouri, California, Colorado, and Indiana. She's married to a retired Army man who now gets to follow *her* around the country. She debuted her first series in 2014 and quickly followed that up with the SEAL of Protection Series, which solidified her love of writing and creating stories readers can get lost in.

If you enjoyed this book, or any book, please consider leaving a review. It's appreciated by authors more than you'll know.

www.stokeraces.com
www.AcesPress.com
susan@stokeraces.com